"As my wife, yo... and privilege,"

Philippe told Nicole. "All of your bills will be paid and you'll have a generous allowance."

"There are names for women who agree to that kind of arrangement," she said sardonically. "*Kept woman* is the most polite term."

"My proposal differs in two important respects. First, we'll be legally married. Second…no sex."

"That's understood. It never entered my mind," she lied.

"I believe I could make it enjoyable for you." His gaze was sensuous as it moved from her face to her softly curved body.

"You're not going to get the chance," she snapped.

Dear Reader,

Our yearlong twentieth anniversary celebration continues with a spectacular lineup, starting with *Carried Away*, Silhouette Romance's first-ever two-in-one collection, featuring *New York Times* bestselling author Kasey Michaels and RITA Award-winning author Joan Hohl. In this engaging volume, mother and daughter fall for father and son!

Veteran author Tracy Sinclair provides sparks and spice as an aunt, wanting only to guarantee her nephew his privileged birthright, agrees to wed *An Eligible Stranger*. ROYALLY WED resumes with *A Royal Marriage* by rising star Cara Colter. Prince Damon Montague's heart was once as cold as his marriage bed...until his convenient bride made him wish for—and want—so much more....

To protect his ward, a gentleman guardian decides his only recourse is to make her *His Wild Young Bride*. Don't miss this dramatic VIRGIN BRIDES story from Donna Clayton. When the gavel strikes in Myrna Mackenzie's delightful miniseries THE WEDDING AUCTION, a prim schoolteacher suddenly finds herself *At the Billionaire's Bidding*. And meet the last of THE BLACKWELL BROTHERS as Sharon De Vita's cross-line series with Special Edition concludes in Romance with *The Marriage Badge*.

Next month, look for *Mercenary's Woman*, an original title from Diana Palmer that reprises her SOLDIERS OF FORTUNE miniseries. And in coming months, look for Dixie Browning and new miniseries from many of your favorite authors. It's an exciting year for Silhouette Books, and we invite you to join the celebration!

Happy reading,

Mary-Theresa Hussey

Mary-Theresa Hussey
Senior Editor

Please address questions and book requests to:
Silhouette Reader Service
U.S.: 3010 Walden Ave., P.O. Box 1325, Buffalo, NY 14269
Canadian: P.O. Box 609, Fort Erie, Ont. L2A 5X3

AN ELIGIBLE STRANGER

Tracy Sinclair

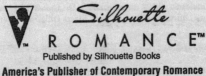

Silhouette
ROMANCE™
Published by Silhouette Books
America's Publisher of Contemporary Romance

SILHOUETTE BOOKS

ISBN 0-373-19439-0

AN ELIGIBLE STRANGER

Copyright © 2000 by Tracy Sinclair

Visit Silhouette at www.eHarlequin.com

Printed in U.S.A.

TRACY SINCLAIR

began her career as a photojournalist for national magazines and newspapers. Extensive travel all over the world has provided this California resident with countless fascinating experiences, settings and acquaintances to draw on in plotting her romances. After writing over fifty novels for Silhouette, she still has stories she can't wait to tell.

IT'S OUR 20th ANNIVERSARY!
We'll be celebrating all year,
Continuing with these fabulous titles,
On sale in April 2000.

Romance

#1438 Carried Away
Kasey Michaels/Joan Hohl

#1439 An Eligible Stranger
Tracy Sinclair

#1440 A Royal Marriage
Cara Colter

**#1441 His Wild Young
Bride**
Donna Clayton

**#1442 At the Billionaire's
Bidding**
Myrna Mackenzie

#1443 The Marriage Badge
Sharon De Vita

Desire

#1285 Last Dance
Cait London

#1286 Night Music
BJ James

**#1287 Seduction, Cowboy
Style**
Anne Marie Winston

**#1288 The Barons of
Texas: Jill**
Fayrene Preston

**#1289 Her Baby's
Father**
Katherine Garbera

#1290 Callan's Proposition
Barbara McCauley

Intimate Moments

**#997 The Wildes of
Wyoming—Hazard**
Ruth Langan

#998 Daddy by Choice
Paula Detmer Riggs

#999 The Harder They Fall
Merline Lovelace

**#1000 Angel Meets the
Badman**
Maggie Shayne

#1001 Cinderella and the Spy
Sally Tyler Hayes

#1002 Safe in His Arms
Christine Scott

Special Edition

#1315 Beginning with Baby
Christie Ridgway

**#1316 The Sheik's
Kidnapped Bride**
Susan Mallery

**#1317 Make Way for
Babies!**
Laurie Paige

#1318 Surprise Partners
Gina Wilkins

**#1319 Her Wildest
Wedding Dreams**
Celeste Hamilton

#1320 Soul Mates
Carol Finch

Chapter One

Nicole Trent's eyes were shadowed as she shuffled through the pile of bills on the kitchen table. How did other single mothers manage to get by on a meager salary? She'd never realized how much it cost to raise one small boy. Especially in an expensive city like San Francisco. Not that she regretted the time and money involved. Robbie was the most precious thing in her life.

Nicole's face softened as she thought about her nephew, asleep in the bedroom. After the accident that had claimed both of his parents that terrible rainy night, she'd made a vow that Robbie would still have all the advantages other children had, no matter what personal sacrifices she had to make.

When the telephone rang, she reached for it without any premonition of the trouble that was approaching like a juggernaut.

A deep male voice with a musical French accent

said, "This is Philippe Galantoire. I wish to speak to Miss Nicole Trent."

The name sent a shock through her. She'd informed this man of his brother's death, out of common courtesy, but she hadn't expected any acknowledgment. Nicole's deceased brother-in-law, Raymond Galantoire, hadn't had any contact with his family for years. She hadn't even known how to contact his brother until recently, almost a month after the accident when she finally got around to disposing of Raymond's things. A scrap of paper with Philippe's address was tucked carelessly among some unimportant papers.

Whatever Philippe Galantoire wanted now, it was too little and too late. Nicole tried to keep the dislike out of her voice as she identified herself, but it was difficult.

"Thank you for notifying us of Raymond's tragic death," Philippe said matter-of-factly.

There was no emotion in his voice, she thought indignantly. He could be thanking her for showing him to his seat at the theater. The man had ice water in his veins! "I realize you hadn't spoken to your brother in five years, but I still thought it was the proper thing to do," she said evenly.

Philippe Galantoire didn't react to her barely concealed hostility. His voice was equally cool when he said, "You mentioned in your letter that my brother left a son. How old is he?"

"He's four," she answered in the same clipped tone.

"What is his name?"

"It's Robaire, although everybody calls him Robbie."

"Where is the boy now? Who is taking care of him at present?"

"He's living with me, but not just temporarily," Nicole said curtly. "He'll be here permanently."

She wondered about all this belated interest. Was this cold, unfeeling man going to offer to contribute to Robbie's support? She could certainly use some help, but not from a person who had considered her sister unworthy to be a member of his family. The Galantoires were fabulously wealthy. They owned vineyards in the French countryside and a winery that produced premium wines and vintage champagne. The money would mean nothing to them. It would simply ease their guilty conscience.

Nicole's jaw set. "I intend to raise Robbie, so you needn't worry about him."

"*You* are the one who need not worry, Miss Trent. I would never permit such an arrangement. The boy is a Galantoire. He will be raised by me and my family."

"I'm not going to let you take my nephew! You're a total stranger! You didn't even know Robbie was alive until I told you." A fact that she was rapidly regretting.

"Unfortunately that's true, but it isn't solely my fault. How could I know? Raymond simply dropped out of sight not long after his marriage."

"What a surprise!" Nicole said mockingly. "All you did was say insulting things about his fiancée and threaten to disinherit him if he married her. Who could take offense at that?"

"I don't have to justify myself to you," Philippe said icily. "Just tell me how soon you can put Robaire on a plane for Paris. I'll make the arrangements and send you an airline ticket. When can he be ready?''

"How about two weeks from never?" she snapped.

"I had hoped we could settle this amicably, but if you're determined to be difficult, I'll just have to—" He paused when he heard a child's voice in the background.

Robbie had come into the kitchen and was looking doubtfully at Nicole. "Who are you hollering at, Aunt Nicky? Is something wrong?"

She put her hand over the mouthpiece and gave the little boy a reassuring smile. "Everything is fine, honey. I wasn't hollering. I guess I didn't realize I was talking so loud. Scoot back to bed, and I'll be there in a minute to tuck you in again."

"I wanna drink of water first."

"I'll bring it to you," she promised. "Just let me get rid of—I mean, let me finish this phone call."

"Okay, but I want it in the glass with Barney on it."

As he left the kitchen, Philippe's voice in her ear said, "Was that Robaire? What is the child doing up at this hour? It must be nine o'clock at night there!"

"It's nine-fifteen, actually," she answered in a flip voice, not bothering to tell this annoying man that she'd put Robbie to bed over an hour ago.

"I don't have any personal experience with children, but I do know little ones should be in bed before now. If this is how you take care of my nephew, it's a good thing I'll be relieving you of the burden," he said coldly.

"In your dreams, pal! Robbie is my nephew, too—

and unlike you, I don't consider him a burden. Forget about taking him back to France because it isn't going to happen!'' Without waiting for a reply, she slammed down the receiver.

Nicole pinned a smile on her face while she gave Robbie a drink of water and a kiss. But when she returned to the living room, her fury erupted.

The colossal nerve of the man! How could he possibly think she'd hand Robbie over to him? After the way he'd treated his own brother, she wouldn't trust Philippe Galantoire with a puppy! The Galantoires only wanted Robbie because he bore the family name. They still thought Sandra was beneath them.

Sandra and Raymond had met the summer she graduated from college. It was in a bistro in Paris frequented by young people. In spite of what the Galantoires believed, Sandra didn't know Raymond came from a wealthy family.

She didn't find out until he asked her to marry him and took her home to meet his mother and brother. Philippe had run the family enterprises since their father died many years before.

Nicole wasn't naive enough to think Philippe would simply drop the matter. His macho pride wouldn't permit a mere woman to make him back off. There was nothing he could do, however. She had as much claim to Robbie as he did.

After a few more harassing phone calls, he'd realize that, think of some excuse to save face and go back to running his empire and chasing girls. According to Raymond, his brother was wildly successful with the ladies.

* * *

By the next morning, Philippe Galantoire was only a vague, unpleasant memory. Nicole's days and nights were too hectic for her to dwell on nonessentials.

She could barely remember those evenings after work when she used to take a leisurely bath and dress in something glamorous for dinner and a night on the town with her choice of escorts. No wonder she'd had more money then. She'd spent almost nothing on food or entertainment and she'd gotten her wardrobe at a discount.

"Look on the bright side. You don't need new clothes every few weeks, even discounted ones," Nicole told herself, grinning wryly as she glanced at her jeans and old, shrunken T-shirt. The front of it was wet where Robbie had splashed her, but it wasn't worth taking the time to change. Nobody was going to see her.

"Who are you talking to, Aunt Nicky?" Robbie called from the bathroom.

"Some overprivileged woman I used to know," she called back. "Don't forget to wash behind your ears." The doorbell rang as she was walking to the kitchen.

"Who's that?" Robbie called. "If it's company, I want to see them."

"Finish your bath. It's probably just Gracie from next door, wanting to borrow something." Nicole opened the door and stared in surprise.

A tall, broad-shouldered man stood in the hall. He was wearing an elegant suit that must have cost a fortune. His thick, dark hair was slightly windblown, but other than that he was impeccably groomed and rather imposing. He had a strong face—high cheekbones, a square jaw and a firm mouth that managed to be severe and sensual at the same time.

They stared at each other for a moment before he said, "I'm looking for Miss Nicole Trent."

She recognized his voice immediately. Philippe Galantoire looked as haughty as he'd sounded. That didn't surprise her, but she hadn't expected him to be such a hunk. Not that it mattered to her.

"I'm Nicole Trent. How did you get to California so fast?" she asked, pulling self-consciously at the hem of her T-shirt. It stopped short of her hip-hugging jeans, displaying a strip of smooth midriff.

Philippe barely heard the question. He was staring at the taut fabric molded to her breasts like a second skin. The wet T-shirt not only outlined her breasts graphically, but her nipples, as well. *Sacré bleu!* The girl had the body of a love goddess.

"What are you doing here?" Nicole asked impatiently. "I thought I made myself crystal clear on the phone. You aren't getting Robbie."

Her curt voice broke the spell. He trained his eyes on her face, deliberately ignoring her sexy appearance. "Did you really think I'd leave it at that?"

"No, I expected you to harass me, but I didn't think you'd be dumb enough to fly halfway around the world on a wild-goose chase."

"You don't know me very well, Miss Trent. I go after what I want. And I don't give up until I get it," he added softly.

"Too bad your winning streak is about to end." Her blue eyes sparkled with anger as she tilted her chin at him defiantly.

"Don't count on it."

They were glowering at each other when Robbie called from the bathroom, "Where are you, Aunt Nicky?" His voice had a quaver in it. "Did you go away and leave me?"

"No, darling, I'm right here!"

She left Philippe standing in the hall and ran to her nephew. Robbie was adjusting well, but he still got anxious at times when he didn't know where she was. Who could blame him? His parents had disappeared without warning. Nicole was all he had left.

Philippe watched her go, running lightly on her bare feet. She was so graceful. With that long, pale-blond hair falling around her heart-shaped face, she looked irresistible.

Philippe took a deep breath. What was wrong with him? Nicole Trent was undeniably sexy and enticing, but he'd known many beautiful women. This one was his opponent. It was crucial to remember that. If she was as smart as she was gorgeous, he couldn't afford to let down his guard.

Setting his jaw, he went inside the apartment and followed the sound of Nicole's voice.

"Bath time is over," she was saying gaily, kneeling beside the tub. "You're going to wrinkle up like a little raisin if you don't get out of the water."

"I wanna be a raisin." Robbie giggled, holding up his arms to be lifted out of the tub. "Then I wouldn't have to take baths anymore, or eat broccoli, or—" He paused, looking past Nicole. "Who's that?"

She glanced over her shoulder and tensed. "Will you kindly wait in the living room?" she said to Philippe. "Or better yet, phone me later on. As you can see, this isn't a convenient time."

He ignored her, continuing to stare at Robbie with strong emotion. "You look like your father," Philippe said softly. "He had dark-brown hair like yours, but his eyes were hazel instead of blue."

"Me and Aunt Nicky and Mommy all have blue eyes. Only Mommy is gone now." The little boy stared at him curiously. "Did you know my mommy?"

"Not very well," Philippe answered in a muted voice. "But I knew your daddy. He was my brother. I'm your Uncle Philippe."

Robbie looked at Nicole doubtfully. "Is he really?"

"I suppose so," she said grudgingly.

"You *know* so!" Philippe said explosively. "First you try to keep the boy away from us, and now you want to deny the very existence of Raymond's family!"

Robbie put his arms around her neck and whispered, "I don't like him."

Join the crowd, she thought sardonically, but she gave the little boy a reassuring smile. "Don't worry, he won't be here long." She lifted him in her arms and turned to face Philippe. "I hope you won't mind showing yourself out. I have to put Robbie to bed."

"I'll wait," he said grimly.

"It might be quite a while. I'm going to read him a story—a long one."

Their eyes dueled as Philippe answered, "Take your time. I'm not going anywhere."

Nicole was careful not to let Robbie see her anger

because it would only have upset him further, but it took effort not to tell Philippe how obnoxious he was. He had no right to come here and disrupt their lives. No way would she let him get his hands on Robbie! He didn't even know how to talk to a child without scaring him silly.

Nicole kept her voice light as she tucked Robbie into bed and discussed what story he wanted to hear. The little boy lost his apprehension once they were alone, and his eyelids started to droop. He fell asleep very soon, unfortunately for her. She wanted Philippe to cool his heels in the living room, getting more bored by the minute. It would serve him right!

After tucking the covers around the sleeping child, Nicole took a moment to change into a dry T-shirt before returning, reluctantly, to the living room.

Philippe seemed to dwarf the small room—as much by his dominant personality as his considerable height. He was standing in the middle of the floor, gazing around disapprovingly.

Nicole was slightly embarrassed as she realized how the apartment must look from his point of view. The dinner dishes were still on the dinette table, and there was a pile of laundry on the couch, waiting to be folded and put away. Robbie's toys littered the floor, and magazines and newspapers were stacked haphazardly on the coffee table.

"I haven't had a chance to tidy up yet," she said defensively.

"Yes, I can see that," he drawled.

Nicole's spine stiffened and she thrust out her chin aggressively. "It's all your fault for barging in unannounced!"

He raised one dark eyebrow. "I'm responsible for the state this place is in?"

"Exactly! You probably have servants to keep your house spotless, but most of us don't. I worked all day, then picked Robbie up at preschool and came home and made dinner. I usually wash the dishes, do the laundry and pick up his toys while he's having his bath. Thanks to you, I'm behind schedule. Call me inhospitable, but I don't have time for uninvited visitors."

"This isn't a social call. If you hadn't hung up on me, we could have concluded our business by telephone."

"As far as I'm concerned, we did," she said flatly.

"You know better than that. Robaire is a Galantoire. We intend to—"

"So was your brother Raymond." Nicole cut him off. "But you threw *him* out of the house. What do you plan to do with Robbie if he doesn't live up to your high standards? Put him in an orphanage?"

"Don't be absurd! Besides, you're wrong about Raymond. He was the one who walked out."

"That's what any decent man would do if someone insulted the woman he loved. Sandra was a wonderful human being. She didn't have a devious thought in her head."

"How could we know that?" Philippe's austere manner lessened for the first time. "They'd only known each other for a short time. Marriage is a big step. We asked Raymond to wait until they were sure of their feelings for each other. Is that so terrible?"

"You did more than advise them to wait," Nicole

said grimly. "You told him Sandra was only interested in his money."

"It's not a unique situation between a girl of moderate means and a rich young man."

"Except that Raymond didn't have any money of his own, yet Sandra stuck by him. Do you have any idea of what a struggle it was for them? Raymond didn't know how to do anything except make wine. The only job he ever had was in your family winery."

"It wasn't busywork for a rich man's son as you imply," Philippe said. "Raymond worked there since he was a boy, learning the business."

"That was actually a hindrance because he didn't know how to do anything else. And Sandra couldn't get a job to help out because of your stringent work rules against foreigners taking jobs. They were reduced to counting pennies—literally!"

Deep lines were carved in Philippe's face. "Raymond could have come to me for money. He must have known I would never have refused him."

"You don't have a corner on pride. Besides, they were young and in love. They treated poverty as a lark. Sandra told me that sometimes they drew straws to see if they should eat dinner, or go to a bistro with their friends, where they'd sit for hours, nursing one drink. They couldn't afford to do both." She had a moment's compunction when she saw the agony on Philippe's face. But he deserved it, she told herself.

"At least I'm glad they were happy," he muttered. "But it didn't have to be that way."

"No, it didn't," she said pointedly.

Philippe jammed his hands in his pockets, tightening the fabric over his muscular thighs. "You think

I'm the villainous older brother who robbed Raymond of his birthright, but you're wrong. I was honestly concerned about him. I loved my brother. I didn't want him to make a mistake.''

"If you loved him, why didn't you try to make up? Is your pride that important?'' Nicole asked scornfully.

"I'm not the monster you think I am. When my temper cooled and I thought his had, I did try to contact Raymond. I left messages, but he never returned my calls.'' Philippe paced restlessly. "After a while, I decided we had to sit down and talk like adults. I went to see him, but by then he had moved from the address I had and I couldn't find him.'' Philippe's hands clenched into fists. "I searched all of Paris, but nobody could—or would—tell me where he was. How could I guess he'd left the country?''

"They didn't have any choice after Robbie was born. The bills were mounting up, and they were only going to get bigger. If they came back here to San Francisco, at least Sandra could get a decent job to support all of them while Raymond trained for some kind of work.''

"Were things better for them here, I hope?''

"Yes, everything worked out great. Raymond developed an aptitude for electronics. He got an excellent job in the Silicon Valley, and they bought a darling little house.'' Nicole bowed her head and looked down at her clasped hands. "Then one rainy night when they were coming home from a movie, a drunk plowed into their car. They were both killed instantly.''

"I'm sorry,'' Philippe murmured.

She nodded wordlessly. The animosity between them had evaporated. Nicole had an inexplicable desire to rest her head on his broad shoulder and let him hold her against his taut body.

"We've both suffered a great loss," he said gently. "And now we both want what's best for their son."

Her moment of weakness passed. Nicole squared her shoulders and prepared for battle. "If you really mean that, then I'm sure you can see that Robbie will be better off with me."

Philippe's expression hardened. "I don't agree. Surely you must admit that a child needs a stable home."

"How pompous can you get? This place doesn't meet your standards because there are a few things lying around?"

"Our definition of 'a few' obviously differs," he said derisively. With a sudden impatient gesture, he said, "This is not the time to argue about minor matters. We have more important things to settle."

"They've already been settled. Robbie stays with me, and you go home and stomp some more grapes so you can make some more money—which is all you really care about."

"What kind of work do you do?" he asked unexpectedly.

The question caught her by surprise. "I...well, I work for a dress manufacturer."

"What do you do there?"

"I do piece work," she answered reluctantly.

Nicole didn't like having to admit she was a low-paid seamstress. It didn't tell the whole story. She aspired to be a dress designer, and this entry-level job gave her an opportunity to observe every aspect of the business. Maybe even get a chance to have some of her own designs considered. But she wasn't going to reveal her hopes and dreams to this arrogant man.

"What difference does it make what I do for a living?" she demanded.

"A lot of difference. Your job doesn't allow you enough time with Robaire. I assume he's placed in the care of strangers all day, so you can only see him briefly at night. And even then you're too busy to give him your full attention."

"That's not true! The quality of our time together is what counts."

"A feeble rationalization," Philippe said dismissively. "At my home in Paris where he belongs, Robaire will have constant care."

"From a nanny whose main concern is her paycheck at the end of the week? I can give him something you can't buy with all your money! But you wouldn't know about anything as unprofitable as love." Her cheeks were flushed with a pink glow, and her eyes blazed like twin blue stars.

Philippe stared at her delicate face in bemusement. If a little boy could evoke such passion, what would she be like in the arms of an experienced man? He was willing to bet she would bloom like a flower, surrendering all of her sweetness to his eager mouth.

Philippe shook his head to clear away the disturbing vision. There was too much at stake to let his imagination run wild.

"That's a very noble sentiment, Miss Trent," he said coldly. "But Robaire needs more than love. He needs a guaranteed future, something the money you despise can provide.''

The argument raged on and on, with neither giving an inch. Finally, Philippe was forced to play his trump card. It was based on a shaky premise, but he gambled that Nicole wouldn't know that.

"I'd hoped you'd cooperate for the boy's sake, but I don't really need your permission to take him back to Paris. Robaire was born in France to a French father. That makes him a French citizen.''

"That's nonsense! His mother was American, so Robbie is as much American as he is French.''

"Not when the place of his birth was France,'' Philippe said in triumph.

This was a nasty surprise. Nicole didn't know if what he said was true, but it was certainly a setback. Even if her claim to Robbie was valid, Philippe had the money to drag the matter through the courts indefinitely. She was just managing to scrape by, with no money left over for a lawyer. The Galantoires would have a whole team of them, all high-priced and eager to litigate.

She decided her only choice was to appeal to his sense of fair play—not a very promising prospect. "I think you're wrong about Robbie's status, but neither of us wants to make him the pawn in a tug-of-war,'' she began in a reasonable tone of voice. "Can't you see how miserable he'd be living with you? He not only doesn't know you, he's afraid of you.''

"I deeply regret raising my voice in his presence, but I assure you, it won't happen again.''

Did he really think she believed that? "Unfortunately, the damage has already been done. Robbie has just lost both parents. You're proposing to take him away from the one person he feels safe with and carry him off to a foreign country to live with strangers. I can't believe anyone could be that cruel to a little child.''

"You do have a point." Philippe hesitated for a moment, frowning. Then his face cleared. "All right, you can come with us and stay until the boy is acclimated.''

Nicole stared at him in outrage. "You're incredible! I'm supposed to quit my job and move halfway across the world just to accommodate *you?*''

"Not for my sake, for Robaire's. If you care as much about him as you keep insisting, you shouldn't have to think twice. As for giving up your job, that doesn't sound like a great loss. I'm sure you can get another one equally as good on your return.''

Nicole was almost speechless with rage—but not quite. "You are without a doubt the most irritating, high-handed, impossible man I've ever met!''

His smile transformed his entire face. Before her eyes, Philippe Galantoire became a charming, devilishly handsome man with a wicked sense of humor. "That's the first impression I often make, but I'll grow on you.''

"Don't bet the château on it," she muttered.

"I'll make the airline reservations," he said as though she'd agreed. "I assume you have a passport.''

Nicole saw a ray of hope. "I do, but Robbie doesn't. He couldn't go with you even if I would permit it.''

"I'll take care of that. The French consul can contact the necessary authorities and expedite the matter. Be ready to leave by tomorrow afternoon.''

"I couldn't possibly be ready that soon," she gasped.

"Nonsense. Call your employer, throw a few things in a suitcase and lock your door. If you forget anything, you can buy it in Paris and send me the bill."

"You think money solves everything!"

"It's never proved a hindrance," he answered dryly.

Nicole had the helpless feeling that she was on a runaway train with no way to get off. If she refused to go, he might get a court order and take Robbie in spite of her. Such things usually took time, but Philippe seemed to know how to cut through red tape. She couldn't let Robbie go without her. The child would be terrified!

"There is a 5:00 p.m. flight to Paris tomorrow afternoon," he said. "I'll book three seats."

"Why do we have to leave so soon?" she asked plaintively.

"Because I have to get back to work. I have meetings scheduled."

"Excuse me for not realizing that," she said with exaggerated courtesy. "I certainly wouldn't expect you to waste your valuable time on unimportant personal matters."

He looked at her impassively. "I'll come for you at three-thirty. Be ready." Without waiting for an answer, he strode out the door.

Chapter Two

Nicole managed to get herself and Robbie packed and ready to leave the next afternoon, mainly by staying up most of the night.

It annoyed her greatly that when he arrived the next day Philippe managed to look well rested and as perfectly groomed as he had the night before, only slightly more casual. This afternoon, he wore a navy cashmere jacket over a white silk shirt and perfectly pressed gray slacks.

She did have to admit that it was nice to have a man ease all the frustrations of travel. Philippe was able to get a skycap when everyone else was clamoring for one without success, and he had already been issued boarding passes. They were flying first-class, of course. Nothing but the best for the Galantoires, Nicole thought cynically.

Robbie was slightly intimidated by the crowds in the airport. He clung to Nicole's hand and ignored

Philippe. But once they boarded the plane, his apprehensions vanished. He was intrigued by everything, especially the earphones that were on the arm of his seat.

As Nicole was taking off Robbie's jacket, a very pretty flight attendant paused on her way down the aisle. The tag on her uniform blazer said her name was Gloria. "May I get you and the boy something to drink after we take off, Mrs. Galantoire?"

She evidently assumed Nicole was Philippe's wife since they boarded together with a child. It hadn't taken her long to find out *his* name, Nicole thought cynically.

"She's not Mrs. Galantoire, she's my Aunt Nicky. And *he* says he's my uncle." Robbie pointed at Philippe. "But me and Aunt Nicky don't—"

Nicole cut him off swiftly. "Come sit by the window so you can watch the planes take off."

Philippe's face was expressionless. When the attendant had gone back to the galley, he said to Nicole, "You're only making it harder for Robaire by showing your dislike for me. I thought we had come to an agreement."

"Like I had a choice!"

"Since you realize you don't, why not make the best of things? If you persist in fighting me, Robaire will suffer the most."

Nicole hated being forced to give in to him so repeatedly, but what he said was true, unfortunately. She'd have to convince Robbie that she liked Philippe—or at least hide her feelings better. What an acting job *that* would be!

After the plane took off, Nicole was able to relax

for the first time. At last, she had nothing to do—except keep Robbie amused, which might not be easy on such a long trip. She put her head back and sighed.

"You look tired," Philippe remarked.

"I guess you might say that," she replied ironically. "Most people have weeks to prepare for a trip to Europe. I had less than twenty-four hours. That didn't leave much time for sleeping."

"Why don't you change places with me and take a nap?" He was sitting across the aisle with no one in the seat next to him.

Before Nicole could answer, Robbie said, "No! I want her here with me."

She couldn't help being gratified. Robbie's dependence on her should show Philippe that he couldn't take her place. But on the other hand, nothing would be gained by alienating him further.

"You have plenty of things to play with," she told the little boy. "I'll be right over there where you can see me."

Philippe watched moodily as she reclined her chair back slightly and closed her eyes.

"Your seat goes back farther than that," he said.

She opened her eyes to see him standing over her. "I know, but I'm not really going to sleep. I'm just going to rest for a little bit."

"You might as well be comfortable while you're resting." He fiddled with the controls on the console until her seat reclined almost flat.

Philippe reached into the overhead bin and took out a pillow and a blanket. After handing her the pillow, he tucked the blanket around her with surprising gentleness. Especially considering how annoyed he was at her, Nicole thought.

"This is as good as being in a bed." She wriggled happily.

His face was expressionless, but her comment triggered an erotic image. He could picture her next to him in bed, relaxed and adorably disheveled in the aftermath of making love.

Philippe straightened abruptly. "Get some rest," he ordered.

That was all Nicole had planned, just a few quiet minutes to herself. But she fell asleep almost the moment her eyes closed.

Robbie refused all of Philippe's overtures when they were alone together, and Philippe had no experience in dealing with a cranky little boy. He was feeling extremely frustrated—something that almost never happened to him—when Gloria came to the rescue.

She brought Robbie a bag of plastic building blocks, one of several toys kept for occasions like this. It was a common occurrence for children to get fussy on a long flight.

The little boy's mood changed instantly, and he started building a tower on the lowered tray table in front of his seat.

"You're a lifesaver," Philippe told her gratefully.

Gloria smiled. "Just doing my job." She had to leave to take care of the other passengers, but she returned intermittently to chat with Philippe. When she found him stretching his long limbs in the aisle, she asked, "Can I get you a drink?"

"No, but I'd like a cup of coffee. I'll come with you." He followed her to the galley.

Through artful questioning, she found out his marital status and relationship to Nicole and Robbie. "What you need is a wife," she said lightly.

"Don't I have enough trouble already?" he answered with a gleam of amusement in his gray eyes.

"You just haven't met the right girl yet." She tilted her head to gaze up at him provocatively.

Nicole woke a short time later and was indignant to see Robbie playing by himself while Philippe and Gloria were chatting outside the galley. The pretty flight attendant was obviously flattered by the attention of such a handsome, successful man. Philippe could be very charming when he wanted to be, Nicole thought in annoyance. He'd even tried to use that charm on her to change her mind about giving up Robbie.

Philippe returned as soon as he noticed she was up. "Do you feel better?" he asked with a smile.

"Not since I found out Robbie has been sitting here all alone," she said distantly.

"He wasn't alone. I just left him for a few minutes to get a cup of coffee. Gloria and I kept him amused."

"I like *her*," Robbie said, stressing the pronoun.

Philippe's face was stormy as he said to Nicole, "Can I speak to you alone?" It wasn't a request.

Nicole stood reluctantly and followed him down the aisle.

When he was sure Robbie couldn't overhear, Philippe said grimly, "I don't care what you think of me, but I object to your making it so clear to Robaire. No wonder he thinks I'm an ogre!''

"Don't blame *me*. Children are a good judge of character.''

His jaw tightened. "Then he'll just have to get used to the fact.''

"Not necessarily. You've only won the first round, not the entire game. It isn't written in stone that Robbie is going to live with you permanently.''

"Don't even think of challenging me,'' Philippe said softly. "I always get what I go after—no matter what it takes.''

As they stared into each other's eyes, Nicole's defiant expression hid the little shiver that ran up her spine. This man would crush anything in his path without a hint of regret. Could she find a way out for Robbie and herself?

The atmosphere was tense between them for the rest of the flight. But when they arrived in Paris, Nicole found it difficult to sustain a grudge.

Although it was the middle of the night, the airport was crowded with people speaking different languages. It was all very exotic and exciting. Philippe took care of the formalities as usual, but this time Nicole wasn't as grateful. After their confrontation on the plane, she was spoiling for a fight—one that she had a chance of winning.

As soon as they'd gone through customs she demanded her passport back. Philippe had pocketed all of them after they'd exited customs. They were in the middle of the baggage section and Philippe was looking around for both his chauffeur and the carousel where the suitcases from their flight would be arriving.

"I'll give it to you in the car," he said.

"How long can it take to hand me a passport?" she persisted.

"I'm slightly busy at the moment, and you don't need it right now. We've already cleared customs." He beckoned to a man in uniform waiting in a roped-off section.

"I want it," Nicole said stubbornly.

Philippe swore in French under his breath, reached into his breast pocket and impatiently pulled out a leather folder. "Here! Are you happy now?"

It was a small victory, but it filled her with satisfaction. She gave him a sunny smile. "Happier than I've been, anyway."

While the chauffeur, whose name was Max, took the claim checks and went to retrieve their luggage, Philippe led Nicole and Robbie to a handsome black limousine parked outside. After only a short delay, Max returned, and the powerful car pulled away from the curb.

When they reached the city, excitement bubbled in Nicole's veins. Her problems with Philippe were forgotten as she gazed at the magnificent Arc de Triomphe set in its own circle like a precious gem. She leaned over Philippe for a better look out the window.

Philippe's own irritation vanished, as well. It was impossible to stay angry when her body was pressed against his, and her cheek was within kissing distance of his lips.

"I should have put you next to the window," he murmured.

"I can see all right."

She put a hand on his shoulder and half turned her body for a last look at the arch through the rear window. Nicole didn't realize their bodies were now in contact from the waist up, but Philippe was acutely aware of the fact. Unconsciously, his arm slipped around her waist.

She gave him a startled look, then drew back hastily. "I'm sorry," she mumbled. "I guess I got kind of carried away."

"Paris will do that to you," he remarked pleasantly.

"Yes, well, it certainly is a beautiful city," she said uncomfortably.

The brief moment of intimacy was embarrassing. She hoped Philippe knew it wasn't planned. He certainly took advantage of it, though, she thought cynically. It was something to keep in mind. Philippe had said he'd do anything to get what he wanted—including making love to her?

The car stopped in front of a handsome town house. In spite of the red and white geraniums blooming in window boxes and the welcoming light over the front door, the house was rather imposing.

The inside was even more impressive. A huge crystal chandelier hung from a high ceiling over a marble-floored entry hall as big as Nicole's living room. In the center was an intricately carved table with a large crystal bowl holding a fragrant floral arrangement.

Nicole caught only a glimpse of a dauntingly formal living room opening off the hall before Robbie distracted her.

"I wanna go to bed," he said.

"I know you do, honey. It's been a long trip."

"I'll show you to your rooms," Philippe said.

As he started towards the staircase, Robbie held up his arms to Nicole. "Carry me."

"I'll take him," Philippe said.

"No! I want Aunt Nicky to do it." As he had on the plane, Robbie again rejected his uncle.

Philippe's face darkened as he watched her struggling up the stairs with the child in her arms, but he didn't comment as he led them down the hallway.

The room he'd chosen for Robbie was tremendous. Everything in it was large—the king-size bed, an imposing armoire, the floor-to-ceiling windows that led onto a balcony. It was so different from his small bedroom in San Francisco that Nicole was afraid he'd find it overpowering. She held her breath, waiting for complaints, but the little boy was too sleepy to notice his surroundings.

"Your room is right next door. I assumed you'd want to be close to Robaire," Philippe added sardonically.

Nicole's room was as spacious as Robbie's, but more feminine. Her large bed was covered with a rose-print coverlet, and the dust ruffle beneath it was made of embroidered white eyelet.

"The bathroom is through that door and a dressing room opens off of it. I hope you'll be comfortable here," Philippe said formally.

"I'm sure I will be." She hesitated for a moment, thinking of how to make amends for Robbie's behavior. Philippe kept trying; she had to give him that. "Robbie was tired, and this is all strange to him.

Don't take what he said personally. He's really a very outgoing child.''

"I'll have to take your word for it," Philippe answered dryly. "If I'm not here in the morning when you get up, the servants will give you breakfast and take care of anything else you need. Paul runs the house, and his wife, Heloise, is the cook."

After he left, Nicole realized how tired she was. She opened her suitcase and took out only a nightgown, not even a robe or slippers. Ordinarily, she would have wandered around inspecting every corner of her luxurious accommodations and then unpacked. But not that night. She couldn't wait to get into bed.

She fell asleep almost the instant her eyes closed. The bed was wonderfully comfortable and the down-filled duvet was warm, yet light as a feather.

Nicole woke with a start when a loud wail pierced the quiet night. Something was wrong with Robbie! She raced to the door and into his room. It was very dark. Only a few rays of moonlight managed to peep through a tiny opening where one pair of drapes wasn't closed tightly.

"I'm here, Robbie!" She raced over to the bed and took the sobbing child in her arms. "What's wrong, darling?"

"There's a great big monster over there!" He clung to her tightly. "He's inside that thing."

"The armoire?" Nicole switched on the bedside lamp. "That's just a big piece of furniture. You put your clothes in there."

"No, it's his cave," the little boy insisted. "He's going to jump out and get me!"

Philippe appeared, looking sleepy. His hair was

tousled and he wore only a pair of black silk pajama bottoms that rode low on his lean hips.

"What's going on?" After Nicole explained, he went over to the armoire and opened the double doors. "See? There's nothing inside," he told the child reassuringly. "You just had a bad dream."

Robbie looked up at Nicole without releasing his grip on her. "I don't care. I don't like it in here all by myself. I want you to sleep with me."

Philippe spoke up first. "I showed you there's nothing to be afraid of. Your aunt will be right next door."

"I want her *here!*" Robbie began to cry again.

Nicole gave Philippe an indignant look, but her voice was soothing when she spoke to the little boy. "Don't cry, honey. I'll stay with you. Lie down and go back to sleep. I want to talk to your uncle for a few minutes. I'll be right outside the door," she added when more tears threatened.

As soon as she and Philippe were in the hall, Nicole turned on him furiously. "How can you be so unfeeling? Couldn't you see how scared the poor child was?

"I tried to reassure him that he was perfectly safe."

"How? By making him sleep in there all alone?"

"He has to get accustomed to it. You can't let a four-year-old set the rules."

"I'm certainly not going to let him lie in that room alone and terrified," Nicole stated.

"That's no problem. Tomorrow we'll move him to another room."

"One as big and forbidding as this one, I'm sure," she said scornfully.

Philippe looked at her austerely. "I'm sorry you don't care for my home, but Robaire will get used to it in time."

"I very much doubt it. You just won't admit that uprooting the child and dragging him over here was a gigantic mistake!" she exclaimed in frustration.

"You've decided that after just a few hours?"

"I knew it all along, but I couldn't convince you."

"You still can't. My nephew is here to stay," Philippe said flatly.

"Even if he's unhappy?"

"That's up to you. If you persist in making me the villain, Robaire and I will never form a bond." He stared at her speculatively. "Is that your game plan?"

"*You* might do anything to get your own way, but I would never stoop that low," she said scornfully.

"That makes it a rather uneven fight, doesn't it?" he asked mockingly.

She couldn't let him know how powerless he made her feel. Lifting her chin, she said defiantly, "I have some secret weapons of my own."

"So I've noticed," he drawled, looking her over appreciatively. "Perhaps I spoke too hastily."

Philippe's insolent manner was a defense mechanism to cover the sudden rush of desire that tingled in his loins once he was aware of her scanty attire. While they were arguing, he hadn't noticed how provocative she looked in the filmy chiffon gown that veiled, yet didn't conceal her charms. He could see that her nipples were the rosy pink he'd imagined they'd be.

Nicole crossed her arms over her breasts hastily, feeling her cheeks bloom with color. She was also aware for the first time of Philippe's near nakedness. His bronze skin was stretched tightly over his taut torso, with no bulges or "love handles" on the lean hips above his low-riding pajama bottoms.

She dragged her eyes back to his face. "You flatter yourself if you think I'd use sex to try to influence you. There are some things that are just too distasteful."

"You think making love with me would be a hardship?" he asked in a deceptively soft voice as he sauntered toward her.

"It isn't the first thing on my list of things to do." Nicole forced herself not to back away although he was so close she could feel the warmth from his body.

"It would be a pleasure to revise your list," he murmured, gazing at her soft lips.

"You'd be wasting your time," she said, but not as forcefully as she meant to sound. Her mouth felt dry as she imagined the infinite ways this man could please her. He would be dominant, yet gentle, arousing her with sensuous caresses until she was twisting with desire in his arms.

Tiny points of light glittered in Philippe's eyes as he gazed at her dreamy face. He put out a hand to touch her cheek, then dropped his arm abruptly. "This discussion is pointless. It's the middle of the night, and we both need some sleep. Go to bed," he ordered.

Nicole felt as if someone had doused her with a pail of cold water. Philippe changed moods faster than a chameleon changed color! One minute he was looking at her with spine-tingling desire, then the next he was issuing orders like a drill sergeant! Not that she wanted him to be amorous. But she wasn't going to let him push her around, either!

"I'll go to bed when and where I please," she flared.

Philippe knew where he'd like that to be. Holding himself rigidly in check, he said, "Fine. Have it your way—why should tonight be any different?" He turned and strode down the hall.

Nicole went into Robbie's room, her body rigid with annoyance. As though she ever got her own way with him! It was impossible to have a reasonable discussion with the man. If he wasn't gritting his teeth in anger, he was trying to seduce her. Did he really think she'd fall for such an obvious tactic?

Nicole was willing to admit that Philippe was a very sexy man, especially with that bare chest and those pajama bottoms that didn't leave much to the imagination. Even she—who didn't even like him!— had responded to his animal magnetism.

That was what was so exasperating! How could she forget, even for an instant, that Philippe Galantoire was the enemy? It was crucial for her to remember that. He wouldn't hesitate to use every advantage against her—and he already had too many.

Nicole walked over to the bed and gazed down at the sleeping child. Robbie's future depended on her. She mustn't let him down.

Philippe was having his own emotional crisis. How had he allowed that woman to slip under his guard? The powerful surge of desire he'd felt had taken him by surprise.

It was just the erotic situation they'd stumbled into,

he assured himself. What normal man wouldn't be affected by the tantalizing glimpse of that exquisite body? For one insane moment he'd wanted to slide those lacy straps off her shoulders and watch her nightgown slither down inch by inch, revealing the nude perfection of her body.

What a colossal mistake *that* would have been! Fortunately, he'd come to his senses in time. He mustn't allow himself to get sidetracked by a beautiful, yet devious, woman who was determined to take Robaire away from him.

Philippe's eyes were somber as he paced the floor, remembering the fateful afternoon five years ago that had led to this impasse. How had the argument with Raymond escalate so tragically? They both had hot tempers, but he was older; he should have made his brother realize he had nothing against Sandra. All he was asking them to do was go slowly, get to know each other better before they took such a big step.

From everything he was finding out, Sandra was a wonderful girl. They could all have had a rich, happy life together if Raymond hadn't cut himself off from his family. Lord knows he'd tried to find him, Philippe thought desolately.

Well, that was all in the past. Philippe squared his shoulders. He'd failed his brother; he didn't intend to make the same mistake with Raymond's son. Robaire was going to live the life he was entitled to—whether Nicole liked it or not.

Chapter Three

Nicole and Robbie slept late the next morning. He was hungry as soon as he awoke, so she got him dressed and took a quick shower before going downstairs for breakfast.

There was no time to enjoy her luxurious pink marble bathroom or even to unpack. She just rummaged through her suitcase for a pair of jeans and a T-shirt.

Philippe's house seemed huge after her small apartment. It was filled with exquisite furniture and priceless knickknacks on every table and shelf. She shuddered to think of the damage a four-year-old boy could do!

Nicole held Robbie's hand as they went looking for the kitchen. Before they found it, a dignified man in a dark suit appeared and introduced himself as Paul, the butler.

When she rather diffidently requested breakfast, he led them to a formal dining room where a long ma-

hogany table was set with linen place mats and delicate china. Heavy damask draped the tall windows,
and there was an elaborate floral centerpiece in the
middle of the table.

After they were seated, Nicole looked apprehen-
sively at the costly Oriental rug under the table. What
a disaster waiting to happen if Robbie spilled his milk
as he frequently did. Wasn't there a breakfast room
in this vast place?

Philippe came in while they were eating. He had
gotten up early and gone shopping. "I bought all new
furniture for your room," he told Robbie. "I think
you'll like it. There's a chest of drawers for your
clothes instead of that big armoire, and I got you bunk
beds. The saleswoman said boys like those." He
smiled ingratiatingly at his nephew.

Robbie didn't glance up from his plate. "I like my
bed at home," he said.

"That's not very polite," Nicole said reprovingly.
She couldn't help feeling sorry for Philippe. He'd
gone to a lot of trouble to make Robbie happy. It
didn't change her personal opinion of him, but he *was*
trying. "Your uncle wants to make you comfortable
here. It hurts his feelings when you act like this."

Philippe gave her a surprised, yet grateful look. "I
would have let you and Robaire select everything, but
I didn't know what time you'd get up. I wanted to be
sure the furniture would be delivered this afternoon."

"I'm sure whatever you picked out will be fine."

"The new chest has to be better than that armoire
anyway. Maybe tonight we'll get an uninterrupted
night's rest."

When Nicole avoided his eyes, Philippe knew she

was reminded of last night's erotic incident. He was sorry he'd mentioned it since she was still embarrassed by it. Although why, he couldn't imagine. She had the body of a goddess.

"My mother is very anxious to meet Robaire," he said to change the subject. "We're invited there for tea this afternoon."

Nicole had no desire to meet Madame Galantoire although she was reluctant to fracture her fragile peace accord with Philippe by saying so. The older woman had been even more adamantly opposed to Raymond's marriage than Philippe had been, according to Sandra.

"I hope Robbie's clothes aren't all wrinkled," she said tepidly. "I haven't had a chance to unpack."

"You have plenty of time. We aren't expected there until three o'clock."

"I have to unpack my own clothes, too. I've been pulling things out at random."

"If you need anything pressed, just give it to Paul." Philippe rose when she did. "I'll arrange to have the furniture removed from Robaire's room. It should be ready for him when we return this afternoon."

After Nicole had unpacked Robbie's suitcases, she started on her own, which didn't take long. The clothes she'd brought didn't begin to fill the large dressing room opening off the bathroom, but she didn't need an extensive wardrobe.

When her suitcase was empty, she dumped the considerable contents of her tote bag onto the bed. A handsome moroccan-leather folder looked out of place among the packets of tissues, the comic books for Robbie and all the other travel paraphernalia.

Nicole smiled, recalling how furious Philippe had been with her when she demanded her passport back. She really should stop trying to irritate him and just accept the fact that they would never agree on what was right for Robbie. She wouldn't change his mind by constantly challenging him—especially over unimportant things.

When she opened the folder to take out her passport so she could return the expensive leather case to him, Nicole discovered that Philippe had given her Robbie's passport by mistake. She skimmed idly over the vital statistics in the little booklet: Galantoire, Robaire Alain. Male. American Citizen.

Nicole's mouth dropped open as she reread those two words. *American Citizen!* Philippe had tricked her! He couldn't have taken Robbie without her permission. That was his reason for rushing them out of the country in less than twenty-four hours. So she wouldn't have time to explore her options.

Nicole's eyes flashed blue fire. If Philippe thought he could get away with this, he was badly mistaken! She was going to demand that he put them on the first plane back to the United States.

Leaving Robbie to play with a deck of cards, Nicole stalked out of the bedroom.

She found Philippe in his study. He glanced up with a pleased smile until he saw the storm warnings evidenced by her pink cheeks and set jaw.

"Is something wrong?" he asked warily.

"Not by your standards. Any underhanded behavior is acceptable as long as you can get away with it.

Forget about how it affects the lives of other people! How can you live with yourself?'' she asked scornfully.

"Would you mind telling me what I'm supposed to have done?''

She threw the passport on his desk. "You gave me this by mistake. Did you think I wouldn't find out you lied to me?''

Philippe gazed at her calmly. "I'd hoped you wouldn't discover it this soon.''

She stared at him in outrage. "Is that all you have to say? No excuses? No apology?''

"I acted in Robaire's best interest. I can provide him with better care and a more secure future than you can.''

"You're wrong, but I won't bother to argue about it because I'm taking him home. If you try to stop me, I'll go to the American Consulate and tell them how you got us here under false pretenses.''

"I might have misled you about Robaire's citizenship, but I have the same claim to him that you do. Your consul can't award custody. That's something for the court to decide—the French court, since the case will be heard here.''

Philippe's message came over loud and clear. The Galantoires were rich and influential in this country. The likelihood of a decision in her favor was almost nil. Nicole was beginning to feel like a small trapped animal.

She eyed the passport on the desk as a solution came to her. Philippe would be going back to work, perhaps as early as tomorrow. When he did, she'd retrieve the passport and search his desk for her own.

Then she'd take Robaire to the airport and catch the first flight home.

As though he could read her mind, Philippe reached over casually and picked up the passport. Dropping it into his pocket, he said, "I'm sorry it was necessary to deceive you, but you left me no choice. In a way, I'm glad it's out in the open. There won't be any subterfuge between us from now on."

"Do you think I'd ever trust you again! As soon as you can get Robbie to tolerate you, you intend to cut me out of his life."

"I'm not the demon you think I am. I've seen how deeply you care for the boy. I just wish you showed the same understanding toward me."

Nicole realized she'd have to compromise or lose her nephew completely. "I'll admit Robbie is related to you, too," she said with difficulty. "I don't want to prevent you from getting to know him, but neither of us wants him to be unhappy. So why don't we try to work out an agreement? What if he comes to visit you for perhaps a month every summer?"

"That's unacceptable," Philippe said flatly.

She hadn't thought it would be that easy. "Well then, let's split his custody—six months with each of us." Nicole hoped she'd find some loophole once she got Robbie home.

"You can't bounce a little boy back and forth across the world like a tennis ball. He needs a stable home, with people willing to take the place of his parents."

"Unfortunately, he will have to settle for less," she answered somberly.

"Not necessarily." Philippe was looking at her

speculatively. "You're not going to stop scheming to get Robaire all to yourself, and I don't intend to let you do it. The discord between us could go on for years, which would be very upsetting for a child."

"That's all true, but what other solution is there?" she asked helplessly.

"We could get married. Strictly for convenience," he added when she stared at him in amazement.

"Is this some kind of bad joke?"

"Not at all. It would solve our conflict—unless you're involved with somebody at home."

"No, there's no one special," she answered, still in shock.

"Then there's no problem. If we were married, Robaire would have the security of two parents who care about him. Instead of fighting over him, we'll raise the boy together."

"I can't believe you're asking me to give up my independence, my job, my whole way of life, just to make *your* life easier!"

"I doubt if even a real marriage could make you give up your independence," he remarked dryly. "You'll still be able to do pretty much whatever you want. All you're giving up is a modest apartment and a mediocre job. As my wife, you'll live a life of luxury and privilege. All of your bills will be paid and you'll have a generous allowance."

"There are names for women who agree to that kind of arrangement," she said sardonically. "Kept woman is the most polite term."

"My proposal differs in two important respects. First, we'll be legally married. Second, no quid pro quo is involved—in other words, no sex," he drawled.

"That's understood. It never entered my mind," she lied. Of course she'd thought about it! What woman wouldn't be affected by that lean, powerful body and wicked charm?

"I believe I could make it enjoyable for you." His gaze was sensuous as it moved from her face to her softly curved body.

"You're not going to get the chance," she snapped. That part was true. This man could be habit-forming!

"Foolish little Nicole." His voice was pure velvet. "Don't you know it's dangerous to challenge a man? It makes him feel the need to prove his manhood." For an instant, Philippe's eyes glowed like a stalking tiger's. Then his expression changed to indifference and he said matter-of-factly, "But it would only complicate matters needlessly if we made love. You have my promise that I'll stick to our bargain."

"We don't have one!" He was doing it to her again. Taking her acquiescence for granted. But this was more important than being bullied into a trip to Paris. "I was completely satisfied with my life until *you* came into it! You don't know anything about me. Yes, my job was mediocre, but it was only a means to an end. I took the job so I could learn every aspect of the dress business from the bottom up."

"You want to be a dress manufacturer?"

"No, I want to be a designer. But you need to know how to do more than just design clothes. Those were the things I was learning. I hoped that when I had a little more experience, somebody at the place where I worked might look at my designs." Why was she telling him all this? Nicole wondered. This arrogant man couldn't care less.

Philippe was gazing at her thoughtfully. "Would you like a professional opinion of your work?"

"Who did you have in mind?" she asked skeptically. Her eyes widened when he mentioned a famous couturier.

"He'll give you an honest opinion, perhaps even some advice on how to get started."

A wave of excitement made her heart beat faster. She'd never even dreamed of a chance like this! If such a famous man liked her designs, it could mean the start of her career!

Philippe gazed in bemusement at her sparkling eyes and softly parted lips. If a simple favor could produce such rapture, how would she react in the arms of a man who could give her more tangible pleasure?

Nicole forced herself back to reality. Philippe's offer was too good to be true. "Why would you do a thing like that for me?" she demanded.

"My motive is purely selfish," he answered calmly. "If you make a new life for yourself here, you'll be content to stay and raise Robaire with me. I'll throw in an added incentive. If you prove to have talent, I'll back you in your own business. I'll even recommend you to all my female friends to get you started."

"You'd do all that for Robbie?" she asked slowly.

He shrugged. "I told you, I don't like to lose."

She didn't believe that explanation. Philippe must care more for his nephew than she thought. As she stared at his strong face, Nicole couldn't help wondering if he could ever care that much about a woman.

"So, do we have a deal? I don't know what else I can add." He gave her a mischievous smile. "You ruled out any of my personal services."

"I haven't noticed that you ever take no for an answer."

"You're a very beautiful woman. Any man would consider it a privilege to make love to you. But neither of us wants to get involved. A platonic marriage will give us both what we want. You can count on me to keep my end of the bargain, for selfish reasons if no other." He gave her a charming smile. "Will you marry me, Miss Trent?"

Her immediate answer would have been a flat, unequivocal no! But once the shock had worn off, she began to consider her options. If she refused his offer, Philippe could—and would—make her life miserable. Whereas if she accepted, Robbie would certainly benefit.

Nicole would never admit it to Philippe, but she realized he could give Robbie things she couldn't, like a secure environment and a good education. She would have done her best, but she could never provide all the child was entitled to. That didn't mean she intended to give up her sister's son, but if she accepted Philippe's offer, she wouldn't have to. No war was won without some compromise. It was either that or lose Robbie completely.

Once her decision was made, it didn't seem so dire. With an impish gleam in her eyes, she said, "Shouldn't a proposal be delivered on one knee?"

"I think a handshake would be more appropriate

in this case." Now that she'd accepted, Philippe was all business. "I'll make the arrangements. Tomorrow might be cutting it a little close, but I think we can be married the following day."

"That's so soon!" she gasped.

"There's no reason to wait. It isn't as if we were having a big wedding with bridesmaids and ushers and all the hoopla."

"That's true. This is just a business arrangement," she said in a brittle voice to cover a nagging sense of disappointment.

Philippe looked at her closely. "I realize this isn't the wedding you dreamed about," he said gently. "If you'd like a big ceremony and all it entails, you can have it. I just thought this might be easier for you since you wouldn't know any of the guests."

"You're right. This is a lot more appropriate under the circumstances." She turned to leave. "I'd better prepare Robbie for the news that he's going to have a new father. I don't think it will be an easy sell."

"Perhaps you can wait until after I tell my mother."

Nicole smiled mirthlessly. "I don't know which of them will take it harder. We'd better postpone our visit until after she's gotten over the shock."

"Mother is very anxious to see Robaire. I'll tell her later this evening, in private."

Nicole wasn't looking forward to meeting Madame Galantoire, and Robbie had to be coaxed into going. The unfamiliar surroundings and the disruption of his normal schedule had changed the sunny-tempered little boy into a cranky rebellious child.

Madame Galantoire lived in an apartment rather than a town house, but it covered one entire floor of the building. Like Philippe's house the apartment was filled with beautiful and costly things.

Catherine Galantoire was an imposing woman with beautifully coiffed gray hair and a reserved manner. She greeted Nicole with chilly courtesy, leaving no doubt that her opinion of the Trent family was unchanged.

Her austere expression altered when she turned to her grandson. "He looks like Raymond," she said softly. "What a beautiful child! Come give your grandmother a kiss, *chéri.*"

Robbie looked up at Nicole, ignoring the bejeweled hand she extended to him. "I don't wanna kiss her," he whispered. "Can we go home now?"

"She's just trying to be nice," Nicole told him in a low voice without looking at either Galantoire. This wasn't her fault, but she knew they'd hold her responsible. She was right about the older woman, at least.

Catherine's cheekbones were flushed with anger. "Don't believe what you have been told about me, Robaire. Come over here to me. I am your grandmother!"

Philippe intervened hastily. "Perhaps the boy would like some refreshments."

He used a bellpull to summon a maid, who responded almost instantly by wheeling in a tea cart covered with an enticing array of food. A fine porcelain platter was covered with tiny sandwiches, and a chafing dish held little puff pastries filled with lobster in a rich sauce. Various petits fours and cookies, all frosted and decorated, filled the three tiers of a silver cake stand.

Robbie was intrigued by the lavish display. He left Nicole's side for the first time and wandered over to the tea cart.

Catherine was delighted. "Here, *mon ange,* let Grandmother help you." She piled a small plate with the seafood puffs and sandwiches and handed it to him along with a napkin.

Robbie took the plate but not the napkin, then bit into a puff pastry that he immediately spit out. "Yuck!" he said, wiping his mouth on his sleeve.

"No, no, *chéri,*" Catherine admonished him. "A gentleman does not spit out what he does not like. You must also use your napkin." She gave Nicole an indignant look. "Is this how you are raising my grandson?"

"This particular situation never came up. It would never have occurred to me to serve him lobster in a sherry cream sauce."

Philippe defused the sticky moment by offering Robbie a miniature éclair. "Try one of these. They were my favorites when I was your age. Remember, Mother?"

A confrontation between the two women was averted, but it wasn't a successful visit. Catherine tried to make up to Robbie, but she hadn't a clue about how to treat a small child. If she ever did know, she'd forgotten. Not surprisingly, he refused all of her overtures.

Nicole was thankful that Philippe had decided to tell his mother in private about his wedding plans. Would he explain to her that it was going to be a marriage in name only? It would take more than that to placate the older woman, Nicole thought mockingly.

She mentioned that to Philippe on the way back to his house. "I don't know how I ever agreed to your proposition. Can't you see it will never work? Your mother detests me, and I have to admit she isn't *my* favorite person, either."

"It isn't necessary for you to be friends," he said dismissively. "We're doing this for Robaire." He lowered his voice. "You'd better have a talk with him when we get home. I made some preliminary phone calls this afternoon and I think we can have the ceremony tomorrow in the early evening."

"Even *you* couldn't arrange things that fast!"

Philippe smiled faintly. "Don't ever make the mistake of underestimating me."

Nicole felt like a leaf being swept over a waterfall. She made an effort to regain control of her life. "Don't think you can make all the decisions and just expect me to go along with them. I should have *some* input. Who is going to marry us and where? I don't intend to leave Robbie at home alone."

The little boy glanced up at her in concern. "Where are you going, Aunt Nicky? I want to go with you."

"She isn't going anywhere," Philippe answered. "We're having a little party at my house and you're invited."

"Is it your birthday? Are we gonna have cake and ice cream?"

"If that's what you want. I thought we'd have the wedding at home," Philippe said to Nicole. "A friend of mine is a judge. He's agreed to perform the ceremony. If you'd like flowers and music, or anything else, I'll gladly provide them.''

"No, that would be foolish since this won't be a real wedding.''

"Mommy and Daddy took me to a wedding once when the baby-sitter didn't show up,'' Robbie said. "I had fun. It was like a great big party. Can I have a birthday party when we go back to our real home, Aunt Nicky?''

"I think this would be a good time to tell him,'' Philippe murmured. When she couldn't bring herself to make it official, he said, "You're going to live here with me from now on, Robaire. Your aunt and I are getting married.''

The little boy gave her a puzzled look. "Mommy said people get married when they're in love. Are you in love with *him?*''

"Well, uh, if we live here, you'll have lots of things you don't have at home,'' she said evasively. "I'll bet your uncle will even buy you that little car you saw at the toy store. The one you sit in and pedal.''

"Wow! Would you really?'' Robbie looked at him with shining eyes.

"We'll go shopping for it together,'' Philippe promised.

Robbie talked excitedly about the car for a while before his attention returned to the intriguing subject of marriage. "Are you gonna sleep in the same bed like Mommy and Daddy?'' he asked Nicole.

"No,'' she answered shortly.

"Why not?''

"Because Uncle Philippe has such a big house that we can each have our own bedroom."

"Nice return," Philippe said with a grin.

"Then how are you gonna have babies?" Robbie persisted. "My friend Kevin says that's how married people get babies. They sleep together."

"I'll let *you* field this one," she told Philippe.

"I don't suppose you'd approve of giving sole credit to the stork?" he asked.

"No, and kids don't believe the cabbage-patch story, either."

Nicole felt her tension lift for the first time as she and Philippe joked together. Maybe their marriage wouldn't be such a disaster after all.

Nicole's apprehensions returned in full force as the day and time set for the wedding approached. Had she made a pact with the devil? Philippe had an uncanny knack of getting his own way. He was even making progress with Robbie!

It had started when they returned from Catherine Galantoire's and found Robbie's room filled with child-size furniture and toys. Philippe knew just what carrots to dangle before which noses, Nicole thought cynically. A career for her and lavish gifts for Robbie.

He was downstairs now, carrying a new stuffed toy and anticipating a party. He couldn't be pried away from her side before this.

Nicole left her room and went slowly down the staircase, hoping she was doing the right thing.

Voices were coming from the den. As she approached, she could see a distinguished-looking older man talking to Philippe while Robbie was happily eating ice cream and cake. He'd had his dinner earlier.

The two men turned when Nicole appeared, and both registered admiration. She just happened to be wearing a white dress although she certainly wasn't trying to look like a bride. It was the only thing suitable in the limited wardrobe she'd brought with her.

The classic A-line dress wasn't new, but Nicole had always liked its simple lines and versatility. For casual affairs she'd often added a cardigan with bright appliquéd flowers. Tonight she wore a short strand of pearls instead. Was the effect too bridal? she wondered nervously.

The two men didn't seem to think so. "You look lovely," Philippe said before introducing the other man—the judge, presumably—as Marcel Lavoire.

He lifted her hand to his lips. "Philippe has always had an eye for the charming ladies. It is no surprise that he picked the most beautiful one to be his bride."

She gave Philippe a puzzled look. The other man seemed to think this was a normal wedding.

"Will you excuse us for a moment?" Philippe said to his friend. He took Nicole's hand and led her to the other side of the room.

"Didn't you explain the situation to him?" she asked in a low voice so they wouldn't be overheard.

"I thought it would be better for Robaire if our bargain wasn't common knowledge. People would be sure to discuss it, perhaps in front of their children, his future playmates. How would we answer him if he asked if we were really married?"

"I guess we could truthfully say yes."

"Are you prepared to answer the rest of his questions? Why we don't share a bedroom, what a business agreement means? If he thinks we don't have a real marriage, he might worry that his life would be disrupted again.''

"But we'd have to pretend..." Nicole's voice trailed off.

"To be in love." Philippe finished her sentence. "It wouldn't be a hardship for me," he said in a husky voice.

When she looked at him warily, his expression changed. Had she only imagined the smoky desire in his eyes?

"Don't worry, I'll only act the role of a loving husband when we're in public," he said mockingly.

"I hate to rush you, Philippe," Marcel called. "But I have another engagement shortly."

Nicole listened in a kind of daze to the solemn ceremony that bound her to a virtual stranger. She wanted to say no and end this charade when the judge asked if she'd take Philippe for her husband. But something stopped her. Sandra and Raymond were as clear in her mind as if they were standing there in the room. They were both smiling and nodding their approval.

Nicole was so bemused that she hardly felt Philippe take her hand. She glanced down to see him slip a beautiful diamond wedding band on her finger.

"You may now kiss the bride," the judge said, beaming.

Philippe took her in his arms and his mouth closed over hers. Suddenly, Nicole's detachment vanished. She was acutely aware of this vibrant man and the way his lips moved sensuously over hers, coaxing a response.

It was useless to remind herself that it was all an act put on to impress his friend. Philippe's warm mouth and lithe body seduced her will to resist. She wanted to clasp her arms around his neck and unleash all the passion underneath that iron control.

When he finally released her and the spell was broken, Nicole was appalled at herself. This whole thing was a terrible mistake that would only get worse! The physical attraction between them had been present from the beginning—even though they disliked each other—but she was no match for this experienced man who would use sex to gain an advantage. It was crucial to remember that in the trying days ahead.

Chapter Four

Nicole struggled to regain her composure after Philippe's arousing kiss. He wasn't the slightest bit ruffled, she reflected bitterly. He was chatting with the judge as though the man had just dropped by to pay a social call.

A few minutes later, Marcel said he had to leave. "I wish I could stay longer, but I'm sure you two can't wait to be alone." He said something ribald in French to Philippe, laughing knowingly. His expression changed to blandness when he turned to Nicole and kissed her hand. "Please accept my best wishes, Madame Galantoire. I know you and Philippe will be very happy together."

After he'd left, Nicole said dryly, "Your friend has an earthy way of putting things. His remark to you was something I'd expect from a high school boy."

Philippe's poise slipped for the first time since she'd known him. "You understand French?"

"I speak it fluently."

"Why didn't you ever say so?"

"I was tempted to when you swore so colorfully in the airport." She grinned mischievously.

"I apologize profusely! I hope you'll forgive me."

She shrugged. "I've heard those words before."

"It never occurred to me that you might be bilingual." Philippe was clearly embarrassed. "I'm afraid I bought into the common misconception that Americans only speak their own language."

"We don't have much opportunity to practice what we learn in school. But when Raymond and Sandra returned to San Francisco, we spoke mainly French together so she wouldn't lose her proficiency. Robbie understands quite a bit of French, too."

"I made the mistake of underestimating you."

"That could be dangerous," she said lightly.

"I'm well aware of it. From now on I'll watch what I say—starting tomorrow, since I don't want to spoil our wedding night." When she gave him a wary look, Philippe smiled faintly. "I was only suggesting that we suspend hostilities during dinner. I thought we'd go to Chez Martine after Robaire goes to bed."

"I couldn't leave him alone."

"He won't be alone. Heloise and Paul will be here with him. She'll sit in his room until he goes to sleep."

Nicole knew that Robbie would raise a fuss. But after Philippe promised to take him shopping the next day for the toy car he wanted, the little boy went to bed without further protest.

"You really have to stop bribing him," Nicole told Philippe after she returned from tucking Robbie into bed. "I realize you can afford to buy him anything he wants, but he's going to become terribly spoiled."

"I'd prefer not to buy his love, but it's the only way I can get either of you to tolerate me. You see, money does have its uses," Philippe added sardonically.

If he thought she could be manipulated as easily as Robbie, he was due for a big surprise, Nicole thought grimly. She intended to be on *her* guard, too.

Philippe didn't act like a man with a secret agenda. The only thing on his mind seemed to be a relaxing dinner in pleasant surroundings.

Chez Martine was one of those elegant multistarred restaurants where reservations had to be made weeks in advance. The atmosphere was urbanely dignified. The tables were set with the finest china and silver, and crystal chandeliers cast a soft light over the smartly dressed people who filled the room with a hum of conversation.

The maître d's hauteur vanished when he hurried over to greet Philippe. "Of course we can find a table for you, Monsieur Galantoire," he said, leading them to a choice spot by a window.

After they were seated and the man had left them alone for a moment, Nicole remarked, "You either come here often or you're a big tipper. I've read that you need a favorable credit rating and three references to get in here."

"It isn't quite that bad. Only two people have to vouch for you," Philippe joked.

They were soon surrounded by an attentive waiter, a busboy and the wine steward. Philippe chose the wine, then dismissed all of them while he and Nicole glanced over the menu.

"Why don't you order for me?" she suggested.

"I don't know what you like." Philippe stared at her curiously. "It occurs to me that we know remarkably little about each other."

"I wouldn't say that. I know you're rich and spoiled, and you know I'm not." She laughed.

His face mirrored her amusement. "Will you admit to being headstrong and hot-tempered?"

"Look who's talking about a bad temper!" she hooted.

"If you're referring to my occasional outbursts, you'll have to admit I was provoked. I believe you do it on purpose."

"You're just not used to anyone challenging your authority," she said lightly.

"And *you're* used to men who will do anything to please you."

"You might try it sometime."

"It didn't get *them* very far. You said you're not involved with anybody." He gazed at her speculatively. "There must have been a lot of men in your life. Have you ever been in love with any of them?"

Before she could answer, the wine steward came to pour the wine. Then the waiter came to take their order, and Nicole again told Philippe to choose for her.

While the two men conferred over the menu, she thought about Philippe's question. The answer was no. She'd never met anyone who made her heart race and her body pulse with desire. Some of the men she'd dated had felt that way about *her,* yet she hadn't shared their passion. It would serve her right if the tables were turned and the man she finally fell madly in love with didn't share her feelings, Nicole thought wryly.

"I ordered some of the dishes the chef is noted for," Philippe said, interrupting her reverie. "I hope you'll like them."

"I'm sure everything here is delicious," she said vaguely. Her mind wasn't on food. "You said we don't know anything about each other, which is true. But at least you know a little about me. Tell me what *your* life is like."

"It's fairly predictable, I suppose. I go to work every morning, like most people. I socialize with my friends. I lead a very normal life."

"Scarcely." She glanced around the gracious room. "Most people don't dine at Chez Martine whenever they feel like it, or live in a mansion."

"I might have more worldly goods, but I'm still a working man."

That was technically true, yet it wasn't the sort of thing she wanted to find out. Since Philippe kept avoiding the subject of his personal life, she came right out and asked him about it. After all, he'd asked about hers. "Some of those friends you see must be women. Is there anyone special in *your* life?"

"Not at the present time."

Had he hesitated before answering? Nicole wondered. It didn't seem possible that a man like Philippe wasn't seeing someone regularly—or that he intended to forgo sex because of their sham marriage. He was much too virile for that.

"I suppose it's fortunate that you aren't involved

with anyone,'' she said. ''You'd have trouble explaining your sudden marriage.''

''Luckily, that's no problem,'' he answered blandly.

''Have you considered the other problems? Marriage is bound to interfere with your, um, normal lifestyle.'' Nicole gazed down at the small plate the waiter had unobtrusively set before her. ''Perhaps you already have a solution. I've heard that some Frenchmen have what they call *une petite amie,* a little friend.''

''How very kind of you to be concerned about my sex life. That *is* what you're referring to so delicately, isn't it?'' Philippe's eyes were dancing with merriment. ''Are you giving me permission to have an extramarital affair?''

''You don't need my permission, under the circumstances,'' she answered coolly.

''There is a way to keep me from straying,'' he said mischievously.

''Don't even think about it! I have no intention of sleeping with you,'' she said in a firm voice.

''You might enjoy it. I would try very hard to please you.'' The flame from the candle was reflected in his eyes as he took her hand across the table.

His low, husky voice sent a shiver up her spine. She could imagine all the ways this sensuous man could please her, from his first arousing kiss to his complete possession of her body.

She pulled her hand away to break the magnetic contact between them. ''This arrangement isn't going to work, Philippe,'' she said, taking a deep breath.

''Because I was honest with you? I'm sure many

men have wanted to make love to you. You're an enchanting woman.''

"If I thought you felt that way, I never would have agreed to marry you!"

"I never heard of a woman being insulted because a man considered her desirable." Philippe chuckled.

"You promised this would be a mock marriage."

"It will be. Nothing is going to happen that you don't want to happen. I think we'd be sensational together, but only if you felt the same way."

"I don't," she said, trying to sound convincing.

The undeniable sexual attraction between them was baffling—and dangerous! Philippe would be a marvelous lover, but his deeper emotions wouldn't be involved. She wasn't foolish enough to think they ever would be, at least toward her.

"I've never made love to an unwilling woman, so you have nothing to worry about. Eat your *petite bouchée* or the chef will take it as a personal affront and we won't be able to come here anymore."

Nicole's attention focused on her plate for the first time. The fluted patty shell filled with crabmeat looked like a picture in a magazine. The crab mixture was topped with an anchovy curl filled with caviar and centered on a small slice of smoked salmon.

"I hope you'll think it tastes as good as it looks. Next time we'll try Celestine's. It's a new restaurant that's gotten very good reviews. Perhaps we'll go there tomorrow night."

"I can't leave Robbie again," Nicole protested.

"Why not? He's in capable hands and he goes to sleep early. Surely you didn't stay home with him every night."

"Actually, I did. It was usually late by the time I finished all the domestic chores, and we both had to get up early the next morning. I was happy just to crawl into bed after everything was done."

"You gave up your entire personal life for the boy?" Philippe asked slowly.

Nicole shrugged. "I just put it on hold for a while. No big deal."

"I doubt that very many women would be willing to make that sacrifice. At least your life will be easier now," he said gently.

"Not necessarily. I won't have to wash dishes or do the laundry but I simply traded one set of problems for another," she said ruefully.

"I don't want to be a problem for you, Nicole."

"It isn't you—although you're the main thorn in my side." Her smile took away the sting.

"I want to make things better for you, not worse. Tell me what's bothering you and I'll fix it."

"Does that include changing your mother's attitude toward me?" she asked ironically. "I don't think even *you* can perform miracles."

Philippe sighed. "I realize that Mother is difficult. She can't accept the fact that Raymond chose your sister over his family. It's illogical to blame you when you had nothing to do with it, but she has to blame somebody besides herself. It must be hell to live with the fact that her last meeting with Raymond ended on such a bitter note."

"I suppose I can understand that," Nicole said grudgingly.

"Robaire is all she has left of Raymond. Mother desperately wants her grandchild's love, but she doesn't know how to talk to him. You'd be doing a real humanitarian service if you could convince Robaire to warm up to her, even a little bit.''

Nicole stared at him indignantly. "Isn't there any limit to what you expect of me? *I* can't perform miracles, either."

"I know it's a lot to ask, but you're the only one who can change Robaire's opinion of her."

"What makes you think she'd welcome my interference? I'm sure when your mother heard we were getting married, she made the eruption of Vesuvius seem like a puff of smoke!" Nicole noted the change in his expression. "Am I right about her reaction?"

"She was a little upset," Philippe admitted. "But she'll get used to the idea."

"I admire your optimism—even if I don't share it. You must have invited her to our wedding, but I notice she wasn't there."

"I know all of Mother's faults, but I can't help feeling sorry for her," Philippe said soberly. "That doesn't mean I'll let her make your life miserable. If she gives you any trouble, I want to hear about it."

"I'm more concerned about how Robbie is going to adapt. It was a good sign that he agreed to stay with Heloise tonight, but maybe I should phone to see if he's all right."

"You can if you like, but she has this number. I'm sure Heloise would have called if anything came up that she couldn't handle."

"I suppose you're right. It's just that this is the first time I've left him." Nicole laughed suddenly. "Listen to us! We sound like a typical young couple worrying about a new baby-sitter."

"It's kind of nice. I think I'm going to like being a family man."

"Wait until Robbie wakes you up in the middle of the night because he wants a drink of water. Or he just gets lonesome and climbs into bed with you and squirms around so you can't get back to sleep. That warm, fuzzy feeling gets cold fast," she said dryly.

"None of those things would bother me." Philippe looked thoughtful. "We entered into this arrangement so Robaire would feel secure. Why not take it a step further? After he gets a little more accustomed to me, I think we should adopt him."

A red flag went up in Nicole's brain. If the situation with Philippe didn't work and she wanted out, it would be almost impossible for her to gain custody of Robbie. Especially in a French court where she'd have to sue. Had Philippe thought of that? Was that the reason he made the proposal?

"I think any talk of adoption is premature," she said coolly.

"It's something to think about."

"Don't push your luck." Her blue eyes flashed angrily. "So far, I've agreed to every one of your terms—against my better judgment and without getting anything in return except vague promises and vaguer reassurance. I don't blame you for thinking I'm a pushover, but I do have limits!"

"I'm sorry you feel I've been manipulating you. I thought I was pretty straightforward about what I'd like from you." He smiled momentarily before becoming serious again. "I freely admit you've been more than generous, but I never made any empty promises. I'll take you to see Jacques, my friend the couturier, whenever you like. Just name the day—tomorrow if you wish.''

"I couldn't be ready that soon. I don't have my sketches with me. I didn't think there was any reason to bring them.''

"Can you duplicate your designs?''

"Yes, but it will take time.''

"Well, just let me know. Whenever you're ready, I'll fulfill my part of the bargain.'' Philippe took her hand across the table and gazed into her eyes. "I'm not trying to take advantage of you, Nicole. I'll admit I tricked you into letting me bring Robaire here, but only because I thought he would be better off with me.''

"You still think so,'' she muttered, ignoring the warmth of his big, capable hand.

"Yes, but you've shown me that he needs both of us. I might not have said it before, but I'm very glad you're here.''

Nicole couldn't help melting in the glow of his eyes and the huskiness of his voice. Was Philippe that good an actor, or did he really mean it?

They were gazing at each other wordlessly when a group of people on their way to a table stopped beside them.

"Philippe!'' a woman exclaimed. "You didn't tell me you were coming here tonight. You just said you were busy.''

"He doesn't have to give you a detailed report of his activities like I do, my dear,'' the man with her—presumably her husband—said.

"How nice to see you, Marie. It was a spur-of-the-moment decision,'' Philippe said blandly. "I felt like having chicken. You might try the roast truffled capon tonight. It was excellent.''

While the others made comments, a blond man was staring admiringly at Nicole. "Aren't you going to introduce your lovely companion? Or are you afraid of competition?''

"I've already beaten out the competition," Philippe said. "I'd like you all to meet my beautiful wife, Nicole.''

Exclamations erupted all around. The consensus was that he was joking.

"Not at all," he said. "We were married this evening.''

"If you're really serious, why weren't we invited?'' Marie demanded.

"It was only a small wedding," Philippe said.

She looked at him with a raised eyebrow. "Another spur-of-the-moment decision?''

"I like to think we were destined for each other.'' He reached over and took Nicole's hand, gazing at her meaningfully. "We knew from the moment we met that we shared a common bond.''

"How *did* you two meet?'' a woman named Helene asked.

"It was totally unexpected," he answered vaguely. "Nicole is...was...Raymond's sister-in-law.''

Their faces sobered for a moment. Raymond had been universally liked. Nicole's connection to him made her all the more intriguing.

After they had all offered belated congratulations, Marie said, "Does Claudine know?''

"Not yet.'' His expression was unreadable. "We

haven't had a chance to tell anyone yet. You're the first to know."

Nicole wondered who Claudine was. Somebody significant in Philippe's life, judging by the looks his friends exchanged. Wasn't it strange that he hadn't mentioned the other woman when she asked if he was involved with anyone?

The group was crowded around their table, creating a traffic jam. The waiters and busboys were having trouble serving and clearing away.

"I guess we should sit down," Marie said reluctantly. "I do want to hear all the details, though. Perhaps the four of us could have dinner tomorrow night."

"We'll join you," the others said in a chorus.

"I'm afraid tomorrow won't work out, but we'll get together soon," Philippe promised.

"I'll call you in the morning after you've had a chance to look at your calendar," Marie said, not letting him off the hook.

After they left, Philippe said wryly, "I'd hoped the news wouldn't get around for a few days, but I should have known we'd run into somebody here."

"It isn't something you can keep secret for long. You must know scads of people in Paris. Why don't you want anyone to know about us?"

"I'm thinking of you. You'll have to pretend to be in love with me. I know how difficult that will be for you."

"You'll have the same problem," she answered dismissively. "We'll manage because we both know it's a charade. We can laugh about it afterward."

"That's the right attitude. It will be our private

joke." Philippe paused as the waiter set a soufflé Jeanette in front of them, a puffy creation of both chocolate and vanilla. He waited until the man had served them and left. Then he continued, "A lot of my friends will want to give parties for us so they can take a look at you and find out everything about you. I don't want you to have to go through that over and over again. It might be easier if we gave a reception and satisfied everybody's curiosity at once."

"I suppose you're right."

"It won't be so bad. They're really nice people. I think you'll like them when you get to know them."

Nicole wasn't convinced that all of them would like *her*. "Who's Claudine?" she asked directly.

"Claudine Duval. She's an old and dear friend of mine. She'll be a big help to you. She's knowledgeable about hairdressers and where to shop, all those things you'll want to know."

"Assuming she wants to be my friend, too," Nicole said skeptically.

"I'm sure you two will get along famously. Everybody loves Claudine. She's smart and interesting, great fun to be with."

It was becoming more apparent by the minute that Philippe had a special attachment to this woman. The question was, why hadn't they ever married?

"What does she look like?" Nicole asked.

"She's a natural redhead, with the green eyes and creamy skin that often go with red hair. Also, a charming little sprinkling of freckles across her nose."

He certainly sounded like a man in love. Whatever made him think Claudine would accept her? "Maybe you should tell her the truth about us," Nicole said slowly. "You can ask her not to tell anyone else."

"The only way to keep a secret is not to tell *any-body*," Philippe said firmly. "Don't worry. After the reception, people will lose interest in us and start talking about someone else."

"I hope you're right."

"Trust me. I'll have my secretary send out the invitations right away. As soon as the party is over, we can get back to normal."

"Whatever that is. Nothing about my life is normal," Nicole sighed.

"It will be," he said soothingly. "Life will just be a little easier for you. For the past few months, all you've done is work and take care of Robaire. You deserve to have some fun, especially at night after he's asleep. I'm going to show you Paris after dark."

Nicole was reminded that she didn't have the proper clothes for an extensive social life. She mentioned the fact to Philippe.

"No problem," he said. "Claudine will take you out to buy a new wardrobe."

"I can't afford the places I'm sure she patronizes," Nicole said bluntly.

"I'll pay for everything, naturally."

"I couldn't let you do that."

"Why on earth not? I'm your husband. I'm legally responsible for your bills. Did you expect to pay for your room and board, as well?"

"That's different."

"I don't see it that way. Please explain it to me."

"I just wouldn't feel right about letting you pay my personal expenses under our present arrangement," she said uncomfortably. "I told you that when you offered before."

"I remember. Would it make it all right if we slept together? I suppose we could change the terms of our agreement," he teased. "I think I could force myself to comply."

"Be serious, Philippe!"

"My dear Nicole, you're being foolish. I'm simply trying to spare you embarrassment. As far as I'm concerned, you would look lovely in a flour sack, but I'm sure you'd prefer to be suitably dressed at our reception and all the other affairs that will come up."

Nicole had to admit he was right. She frowned in concentration. "Do you think I could rent a sewing machine? I don't suppose you have one."

He gave her a wary look. "You want to make your own clothes?"

"Don't look so shocked." She couldn't help laughing. "I did make my living as a seamstress and I do plan to be a designer. It would be wonderful exposure. I'd have a chance to show off my original creations."

"If that's what you want," he said reluctantly.

"Don't worry." She grinned, echoing his earlier advice. "They'll almost have to be better than a flour sack."

The house was quiet when they returned home. The servants had left lights on downstairs so it felt welcoming, but the household had retired for the night.

"Would you care for a nightcap before turning in?" Philippe asked.

She shook her head. "I've already had more to

drink than usual. Thank you for the wonderful dinner. I had a very nice time."

"You sound surprised." He chuckled as they walked up the stairs together. "I told you I'd grow on you."

"That's because we didn't argue all evening," she said lightly.

"We did, but you won all the arguments."

"Only the last one, which you didn't really care about." When he stopped in front of her door, she said, "I'm going to check on Robbie."

"I'll go with you."

The little boy was sound asleep, curled up with a teddy bear in his arms. Nicole straightened his bunched-up covers before bending down to kiss his cheek.

"Could I...?" Philippe asked hesitantly.

"Of course." She was touched by the yearning on his face.

He gently brushed back the child's silky hair, then kissed his forehead. Nicole felt reassured. She and Philippe had perhaps irreconcilable differences, but they shared one bond. They both loved their nephew.

After they'd tiptoed out of the room and paused to say good-night, she could feel the mood between them change. They were suddenly very much aware of each other.

"Well, uh, I guess I'll go to bed," she said. "It's been a very eventful day."

"Cheer up, the worst is over. Who knows? You might even find you like being married." Nicole tensed as his head dipped towards her, but Philippe merely cupped her chin in his palm. "You look tired.

Get some rest, *chérie*.'' He kissed her cheek and went down the hall to his bedroom.

Her skin still tingled from his warm mouth as she went into her own room. The situation was provocative; they were married, yet not married. That was the only reason her nerves were jangled, she told herself. It was only natural to imagine how different her wedding night could have been if she indulged in sex as casually as she was sure Philippe did.

He would be here with her now, undressing her slowly, arousing her with tantalizing caresses as he unzipped her dress. She could almost feel his long fingers stroking her breasts, his wet tongue curling around her aching nipples.

Nicole drew in her breath sharply, trying to blot out the erotic image. She was playing right into Philippe's hands! This was what he was counting on. That the chemistry between them would flame out of her control. But he was wrong. She was never going to let that happen!

Chapter Five

Nicole was enjoying the luxury of sleeping late the next morning when Paul woke her to say she had a telephone call.

It had to be Philippe; she didn't know anybody else in Paris. Nicole picked up the phone with a strange rush of anticipation.

A furious female voice greeted her. Without any preamble, the woman said, "Did you think I would let you get away with this outrage? I'll have the marriage annulled! We both know you're only after Philippe's money, but I'll see to it that you don't get one sou!"

"Madame Galantoire, I presume," Nicole said tightly. "I didn't expect congratulations, but you're angry at the wrong person. Take it up with your son. Philippe was the one who insisted on this marriage."

"That's a lie! You trapped him the way your sister trapped my Raymond. You're both cheap opportunists. I've heard about your kind of woman. You tease and tantalize a man until he has to have you at any cost.''

Nicole's eyes narrowed dangerously. ''You can call me any names you wish, but you can't talk about my sister like that. She gave Raymond more love and happiness in their short time together than he'd ever known before. If you really cared about him, you'd be grateful to Sandra instead of vilifying her.''

''How dare you talk to me like that?''

''Somebody should have a long time ago,'' Nicole muttered.

''What do you know about a mother's love? Your sister stole Raymond from me, and now you're trying to take Philippe and my grandson.'' The older woman's voice was anguished.

This spoiled, intolerant woman didn't deserve consideration, but Nicole did feel a twinge of pity. ''I'm not trying to come between you and your son,'' she said more gently. ''You have nothing to worry about.''

''If you really mean that, you'll go back where you came from and leave us alone. I'll give you money,'' Catherine said eagerly. ''Just stay away from my loved ones and you can name your own price!''

''Do you honestly think I'd sell my sister's child to the highest bidder?'' Nicole asked disgustedly. ''You must be a very sick woman.''

''Don't be a fool! You'll wind up with nothing. When Philippe gets tired of you, he'll turn you out without a penny.''

''Then save your money. All you have to do is wait,'' Nicole drawled.

"You're confident now, but time is on my side," Catherine said furiously. "I'm going to be watching and waiting for you to make a mistake. Greedy women like you always do. And when I catch you, you'll be sorry you ever heard of the Galantoires."

"I already am. Goodbye, Madame Galantoire," Nicole said firmly, cradling the receiver.

She'd kept her voice level, but she was shaking after the ugly confrontation. Nobody had ever hated her before or been that abusive. Nicole's first angry impulse was to confront Philippe and suggest he put a muzzle on his mother. Then she had second thoughts.

He would be caught in the middle and it wouldn't change anything. He already knew his mother was difficult; talking to her wouldn't help. It might even cause a rift between them, which would be sad. Philippe was all the older woman had left. She was a flawed human being, but even disagreeable people had feelings. Nicole sighed.

That wasn't her only problem as the day progressed. She was having trouble keeping Robbie amused. Philippe had bought him the car he promised, then he dropped him at home and went off to work. Robbie was ecstatic with his new toy—until the novelty wore off. Then he trailed after Nicole, complaining that he had nothing to do. She didn't have a moment to herself.

When Philippe returned from work that evening, he took one look at her set face and sighed. "I'm sorry about Mother's phone call today."

Nicole was momentarily startled out of her annoyance. "What did she tell you?"

"Enough to know that she was inexcusably rude to you. We had a long talk and I took care of the matter," he said grimly. "She won't bother you again."

"I'm sorry she told you. I hope you didn't say anything you'll be sorry for."

He gave her a puzzled look. "My mother's behavior was unacceptable. From what I gather, she was thoroughly unpleasant. Why should you care if we argue?"

"Nothing you say will change her opinion of me. We'll never be friends or even like each other. But I can imagine how terrible it would be to lose a son, especially one you were estranged from. And on top of that, to have to worry about losing your remaining son, which is what she's afraid of."

Philippe stared at her in silence for a moment. When he answered, his voice was husky. "That's remarkably understanding. I'm afraid the Galantoires haven't been as generous toward you."

"It's never too late," she said lightly to hide her pleasure. She hadn't expected Philippe to be this solidly on her side.

"Just tell me what I can do for you."

"Nothing for me, but I need to talk to you about Robbie. He doesn't have anybody to play with or anything to do all day. It's not a healthy atmosphere."

"I've been thinking about that. I realize a town house isn't the best place to raise an active boy. He needs fields to run in and pets to romp around with."

"That would be ideal. Where do we find them?"

"At my château in the country. We'll pack up and move there. We have horses and dogs, and I have friends with children on neighboring estates. It's a youngster's paradise."

Nicole felt a slight pang at leaving Paris. She'd caught only a glimpse of the exciting city. But Robbie's needs were more important. "That sounds like a perfect solution, but what about your work? Will you be able to come visit on weekends?"

"Do you think I could be separated from you for a whole week?" As Nicole felt a glow of pleasure, Philippe continued, "What would people think? We're newlyweds. I'll simply work out of my office at the winery."

"That's convenient. How soon can we move?"

"Right after the reception."

It was more than two weeks away! "What will I do with Robbie for that long?" Nicole asked despairingly. "I had trouble keeping him busy for one day!"

"Let me worry about that." When she looked doubtful, Philippe said, "I want you to relax and enjoy yourself. You've given up enough for Robaire."

"I never considered it a sacrifice."

"I know. That's what makes you so special," he said in a husky voice.

Nicole was surprised—and disturbed—by the happiness his compliment brought. Philippe was expressing gratitude, nothing more, she told herself. Underneath that handsome, charming exterior was the same hard-as-nails man she'd first met. It was important to remember that.

Philippe put his hands on her shoulders. "Let me share some of the responsibility, *chérie*. You aren't alone anymore."

She hadn't had anyone to lean on for so long, not

since her parents died many years ago. It was a nice feeling to have somebody to share with. She gazed into his eyes, almost wishing he'd put his arms around her and hold her close.

Philippe drew in his breath sharply as he gazed at her softly parted lips. His head dipped toward hers and Nicole was powerless to move away.

But at the last moment, his hands dropped to his sides and he moved back, murmuring, "I'm sorry."

She felt as if she'd been doused with a pail of cold water—something she needed, Nicole told herself bitingly. How many more ways could this man tell her he didn't want to get involved? Courtesy wasn't the same as caring.

Philippe had recovered his poise almost immediately. "I'll locate a good nursery school for Robaire, and Paul can drive him there and pick him up. Robaire will be happy, and you'll finally have some time to yourself."

"I would like to rent a sewing machine and go shopping for fabric," she admitted. "I have to make a dress for the reception, and there isn't much time."

Philippe had a wonderful ability for getting things accomplished swiftly and seemingly without effort. He contacted some of his friends who had children and found a nursery school that met with Robbie's enthusiastic approval.

Nicole didn't have to rent a sewing machine. Philippe took care of that, as well. He bought one for her and had it delivered the next day, then turned an upstairs bedroom into a sewing room for her.

She was hard at work on her dress a couple of days

later when Philippe came home unexpectedly at noon to take her out for lunch and shopping.

"I already bought some fabric and I don't need anything else." She showed him a length of champagne-colored silk. "This is for the dress I'm making. Do you like it?"

"Yes, it's lovely. You do need something else, though. We have to pick out your engagement ring."

"Is that really necessary, Philippe? It seems like such a needless expense."

"It's all part of the window dressing. My friends didn't notice you weren't wearing a ring the other night because they were too surprised at the news of our marriage. But they'll certainly notice at the reception."

Nicole was getting tired of being reminded that she was merely a useful prop to Philippe. Not that she wanted theirs to be a real marriage, but it would be nice if he realized she was a person, too.

"You don't need me to go with you. Whatever you select will be fine."

He slanted a look at her, alerted by her tone. "Choosing an engagement ring is something a man and a woman should do together," he said in a voice like melted honey.

"You're talking about a normal couple. Nothing about our relationship fits that description."

"Do you want it to, Nicole?" he asked softly.

"Certainly not! No more than you do." She turned her back and started putting pins at random into the soft fabric.

Her body stiffened as she sensed him moving

closer, but she didn't turn around. She didn't see the look on his face or the hand lifted to touch her hair.

After a moment, Philippe's hand dropped to his side and he said casually, "I'll see you tonight, then, if you're sure you don't want to go with me."

The dress Nicole had designed for their reception was everything she'd hoped it would be—simple, yet elegant. The long gown was cut on the bias, so it flowed smoothly over her body. The spaghetti straps left her shoulders almost bare, and the cowl neckline was provocative without being plunging.

She spent a lot of time on her makeup that night, applying blush and lip gloss so artfully that they looked natural. Her hairdo was simple, yet glamorous. She brushed her blond hair until it gleamed like a length of satin, then let it float long and straight around her shoulders. When she was finished, Nicole was satisfied that at least she looked the part of a wealthy man's wife.

Although she had confidence in her appearance, Nicole was slightly nervous about meeting Philippe's friends. Would they accept the reason for their whirlwind marriage?—that they'd fallen in love almost instantly. It was going to make their playacting that much harder.

Philippe's reaction was more than satisfactory. "You look sensational!" The flash of desire in his eyes told her he wasn't merely being polite. "I can't believe you made that gown yourself."

"I told you I was talented. You thought I was going to disgrace you tonight," she teased.

He took her hand and brought it to his lips. "You

would be an asset, *chérie*, no matter what you had on.''

To hide her pleasure, she asked jokingly, ''Are you rehearsing your part as the ardent bridegroom?''

''Everything I say isn't calculated,'' he chided. ''I wonder if you'll ever trust me.''

''I could say the same about you. We're not your average bride and groom.''

''If I ever start to forget, I can always count on you to remind me,'' Philippe answered dryly. ''The guests should be arriving at any moment, so you'd better put this on.'' He handed her a blue velvet jeweler's box.

Inside was a large, square-cut emerald ring. It was so magnificent that she gasped. The flawless green stone was surrounded by flashing diamonds that enhanced its brilliance.

''It's gorgeous, Philippe, but surely you didn't have to make such an extravagant gesture. This must have cost a fortune!''

His mouth twisted sardonically. ''I wanted to be sure *my* devotion looks convincing, at least.''

Why did tension always spring up between them? Nicole wondered despairingly. Philippe's admiration had seemed genuine, but a few moments later there was veiled hostility between them. What did he want from her?

When the guests started to arrive, Nicole was too busy to worry about her relationship with Philippe. She met so many people that she finally gave up trying to remember all of their names.

As expected, his friends looked her over covertly, trying to see what special something had attracted the most eligible, yet elusive, bachelor in their group.

They asked endless questions, as well. Not only about how they met, but also what future plans they'd made.

"Where are you going on your honeymoon?" Marie Dupuis asked. She and her husband Georges were the couple from Chez Martine.

Nicole let Philippe field the question since it was one they hadn't anticipated.

He put his arm around her waist, saying, "We haven't decided where we want to go yet. We've been too busy getting to know each other."

"I can't think of a better place than on a honeymoon. Ours was so romantic. We went to Tahiti." A woman named Claire sighed happily.

"Nicole and I don't have to go anywhere to find romance." Philippe tipped her chin up and looked at her adoringly.

Her body tensed in spite of her effort to look relaxed. Nicole was tinglingly aware of his caressing fingers on her skin and his muscular thigh pressing against hers. Philippe was an awesome actor. She could almost imagine—like his audience—that they spent their nights making passionate love, their nude bodies glistening in the moonlight as they moved erotically against each other.

"That's so poetic." Marie turned to her husband. "Why don't you ever say lovely things like that to me?"

"They're newlyweds," he answered. "Wait until they've been married for a few years. They'll settle down like the rest of us."

"You're wrong, Georges," Philippe said softly. "The magic between us will only grow, won't it, my angel?"

"Yes," Nicole murmured, mesmerized by his throaty voice and the desire in his eyes.

They stared at each other, oblivious to the people around them.

The spell was broken when one of the men complained, "You're making life difficult for the rest of us, Philippe."

"Or perhaps I've given you an incentive to put romance back in your marriages," he answered lightly. As he led Nicole to the next group of guests, he said, "I believe I handled that rather well, don't you?"

"I thought you overdid it," she replied coolly, pulling her hand away from his. "You sounded like a lovesick schoolboy."

"That's the way love is supposed to make you feel. But I was talking about the way I deflected questions about our honeymoon. You have to admit *that* was masterfully done."

"I thought my performance was better," she said, ignoring the fact that her response hadn't been faked. "Don't I deserve some credit, too?"

"You should have been an actress. You almost fooled *me*," he said mockingly. He took her hand again as they were joined by other guests.

Philippe was charming to everyone, but his face lit up when he spotted a late arrival, a stunning redhead. She had on a green satin gown and a spectacular emerald-and-diamond necklace. Claudine Duval, without a doubt.

"There's Claudine. Come, I want you to meet her." Philippe led Nicole across the room. After introducing the two women, he said to the redhead,

"You're more than fashionably late. I was afraid you weren't coming."

She kissed him on both cheeks. "How could I pass up an opportunity to meet the woman who finally tamed the wild stallion, *chéri?*"

"That's scarcely an apt description," he protested.

"Who knows you better than me?" She grinned mischievously. Turning to Nicole, she said frankly, "I suppose you realize everyone is wildly curious about you."

"Yes, I guess I should have prepared a résumé," Nicole said, trying for a light tone.

The woman had made her relationship with Philippe crystal clear. Was her frankness a warning that she didn't intend to call off the affair? That seemed rather tacky. Not that she cared, Nicole assured herself. But she had hoped the two of them would at least be discreet.

"As an American, do you think you'll like living in France?" Claudine asked.

"I'd prefer to live in San Francisco, but Philippe is very persuasive." Nicole slanted a glance at him, which he ignored.

"I told Nicole you'd help her with all the things I can't," he said to Claudine. "Like where to have her hair done, things like that."

"I'd be happy to. I'll also take you to a little shop I discovered that carries stunning clothes when you need something right away," she said to Nicole. "Couturiers always require so many fittings."

Nicole was surprised when Philippe said, "That's one thing she doesn't need. Nicole has golden fingers. She made the gown she's wearing tonight."

"He's joking, isn't he?" Claudine looked her over appraisingly. "That gown is positively stunning! I can't believe you made it."

Some women standing nearby heard her and joined in the inspection. The comments were all favorable, but so was the disbelief.

"I'll bet you just told Philippe it was your own creation so he wouldn't know how much you paid for it," a woman named Simone joked.

Philippe put his arm around Nicole. "We don't have any secrets from each other," he said suavely. "Our marriage is based on trust, is that not so, *chérie?*"

"And a lot of faith," she replied ironically.

Claudine was watching them with narrowed eyes, but the other women were more interested in Nicole's gown. As they asked questions about how she learned to sew so divinely and was it her original design and so forth, Philippe and Claudine moved away unobtrusively.

Nicole managed to answer their questions while watching the other couple obliquely. They didn't leave the drawing room, but their absorption in each other made it clear that they didn't welcome company. Claudine was talking earnestly to Philippe, and it looked to Nicole as though he was reassuring her of something.

That his marriage wouldn't affect their relationship? Nicole was coldly angry. Not that she really cared, but Philippe might have had the decency to keep up appearances at their wedding reception!

When an attractive man joined the group around her and expressed his obvious admiration, she was more receptive than she might have been. His name was François Clermont and he said he was an old friend of Philippe's.

After a few moments, he deftly drew her away from the others and over to the tall French windows where they could be alone.

"We were all amazed to hear Philippe had finally married, but after seeing you, I find it understandable," François said gallantly. "I only wish I had met you first."

"I think Claudine wishes you had, too," Nicole answered lightly. "She and Philippe seem to have a close rapport."

"They've always had a special kind of friendship, but his marriage needn't change that."

Nicole smiled brightly. "I guess I have a lot to learn about the French."

His expression changed. "I'll be glad to teach you anything you want to know," he murmured.

Philippe materialized at her side. He was smiling, but his eyes were cool. "Whatever François is telling you, don't believe him."

"I was just trying to make your lovely bride feel welcome," François said.

"And I certainly appreciate it," Nicole said warmly for Philippe's benefit.

"If you'll excuse us, I want to talk to my wife," he told the other man, taking her arm in a firm grasp. When they were out of earshot, Philippe said in an annoyed tone, "This is scarcely the proper time to flirt with François. We're supposed to be acting like a happily married couple."

"Is that what *you* were doing when you went off in a corner for a private chat with your girlfriend?"

"It's not the same thing. I told you Claudine is an old friend."

"It's exactly the same thing, except François is a *new* friend."

Philippe's jaw set grimly, but before he could explode, Paul coughed discreetly. The butler had been hovering in the background, waiting to announce that the buffet supper was ready.

Nicole and Philippe didn't have a chance to talk privately until the party was over. By then, he'd forgotten his annoyance with her. "I think the evening went well," he said after the last guests had departed. "We were quite convincing, don't you think?"

"I suppose so."

"I tried to do *my* part," he said mischievously.

"Except for one noticeable lapse."

Philippe's laughter faded. "I had hoped you and Claudine would be friends."

"I'm willing to overlook your affair, but asking me to be friends with her is a little too much to ask," Nicole said tartly.

"You're starting to sound remarkably like a wife."

"I'm willing to call it off any time you are."

After a look at her stormy blue eyes, Philippe became conciliatory. "You're tired, *chérie*," he said in a honeyed voice. "Meeting so many strangers all at once is an ordeal. But everything will be easier from now on, I promise." He lifted her hand to his lips. "Get a good night's rest, my dear."

Nicole was tired, but she couldn't fall asleep. Why did it bother her that Philippe intended to continue his affair with Claudine? She couldn't expect a man as virile as he was to remain celibate. What difference did it make whom he slept with?

But it did matter. What she'd experienced when she saw them together felt frighteningly like jealousy. But that couldn't be! She wasn't in love with Philippe.

Nicole sighed and wedged the pillow under her cheek. She was just being a dog in the manger. She didn't want Philippe but she didn't want anyone else to have him. That explanation should have satisfied her, but it didn't.

Chapter Six

Nicole was dazzled by her first glimpse of Philippe's country estate. The imposing château looked like a castle set in the middle of velvety green lawns bordered by a forest in the distance.

As soon as Max stopped the limo in front of the massive double front doors of the house, two large dogs dashed up to greet them, wagging their tails frantically.

"Do they live here?" Robbie asked Philippe excitedly. "Are they yours?"

Philippe nodded and said, "They're yours now, too."

Robbie gave him an ecstatic look and fumbled impatiently with the car door.

A tall, rangy man had followed the dogs. He was accompanied by a small boy about Robbie's age. Philippe introduced the man as Maurice, the groundskeeper, and the child as his son, Jules.

While Maurice was offering his best wishes for their marriage the two little boys were silently sizing each other up. They seemed to come to a favorable conclusion because Jules offered to show Robbie a litter of puppies down by the servants' quarters.

"Can I go see them, Aunt Nicky?" Robbie asked eagerly. "Please, please!"

"I'll look after the young master," Maurice offered.

When Nicole gave her consent, the two little boys took off across the lawn with the dogs frolicking and barking around them.

"That's the happiest I've ever seen him," Philippe remarked wryly as he and Nicole walked toward the house.

"He's usually like that. I think he'll be a lot more content here, now that he has somebody to play with."

When they went inside, the entire staff was lined up in the huge entry hall to greet the new mistress of the house. Since the château was the size of a modest hotel, it took a small army to run the place. Besides Paul and Heloise, who had driven down in another car, there were innumerable maids and a sprinkling of young men whose duties Nicole couldn't even imagine.

Philippe laughed at the dazed look on her face as he led her upstairs after the introductions. "Don't worry. You'll learn all their names in time."

"I hope so, but my experience in dealing with a staff is limited. At home, *I'm* the household help."

"This is your home now, and you won't have to lift a finger."

Philippe's satisfied smile disturbed her somehow. He could afford anything he wanted. Had he bought her, as well?

Nicole's troubling thoughts were driven from her mind when Philippe showed her the master suite. The king-size bed seemed dwarfed by the huge room, which also had a couch and several comfortable chairs in front of a fireplace at one end.

It was an unmistakably masculine room. The dark-blue bedspread and the heavy drapes looped back from the tall French windows were tailored, and there were no knickknacks scattered around on tables, only books and a few photographs in silver frames.

One was of Raymond and another was of Claudine, Nicole noticed. She wondered acidly if he intended to put it in a drawer, now that he was technically a married man.

"This is very nice. You can tell it's a man's room."

"The color scheme doesn't suit you?" His expression was innocent, but his gray eyes danced impishly. "Feel free to redecorate any way you like."

"You know perfectly well that I don't intend to share this room with you."

"Women have been known to change their minds," he teased.

She ignored his remark, frowning. "We have a bit of a problem. What are the servants going to think when we don't share the same bedroom?"

"They're not likely to question me about it. If we keep up our devoted-newlywed act, they'll simply assume that one of us snores."

"I suppose I'll have to be the culprit since I doubt

if any of your other companions complained." Before he could comment, she asked, "Where is my room?"

"Right through here." He opened a connecting door into another equally elegant suite.

Nicole didn't notice immediately. She was too focused on the implications of the unlocked door.

Philippe was aware of her reservations. "There's a limit to what you can expect the servants to swallow. Many couples have separate bedrooms for one reason or another, but they don't put padlocks on the doors. I can assure you that I have no intention of creeping into your bed in the middle of the night to ravish you. An unwilling woman holds no charm for me."

Nicole felt extremely foolish. A man like Philippe wouldn't have to use force—or even much persuasion. "That never even crossed my mind," she lied, turning hurriedly to survey the room. "This is charming!"

That, at least, was true. The furniture in the light and airy bedroom was more delicate than Philippe's solid pieces. It was upholstered in pastel prints with lots of throw pillows. And instead of heavy drapes, sheer lace curtains billowed in the breeze from French doors that opened onto a balcony overlooking a beautiful garden.

"I hope you'll be comfortable here. Your bath and dressing room are through there." He indicated a door on the opposite wall. "I told Paul to have the suite prepared for you. He's pretty efficient, but if you need anything, just tell either of us."

"I can't imagine what else I could need."

"Well, I'll let you get unpacked."

Nicole didn't have that much to unpack, so she

explored her quarters instead. The dressing room was as large as a small bedroom. It had endless drawers and shelves, as well as hanging space for every kind of garment, and a shoe rack that had space for more shoes than she'd ever owned.

But the pièce de résistance was the bathroom. In the center was a sunken marble tub with faucet handles made of rose quartz. There was also a shower with clear glass panels. One long wall of the room was mirrored, reflecting the incredible luxury.

Nicole had always known Philippe was rich, but she hadn't realized just how wealthy he must be. The château was probably hundreds of years old, so it must have cost a fortune to modernize the interior like this. And how beautifully it had been done, without losing any of its old-world charm.

Nicole smiled as she glanced again at the sunken tub. Robbie wouldn't have to be coaxed to take a bath anymore. That reminded her that she didn't know where his room was located.

She went back into the bedroom and across to the connecting door. The door was closed, but the latch hadn't caught, so when she knocked, the door swung open. Nicole was frozen to the spot as Philippe came out of the bathroom stark naked!

He was drying his hair vigorously with a bath towel, so he didn't see her at first. When he did, Philippe was as startled as she was. They stared at each other for a quivering moment that seemed to last an eternity.

Nicole was aware of every inch of his lean, totally masculine body. It was as perfectly sculpted as a classical statue of a Greek athlete. But Philippe was very human. His body radiated virility. Her eyes were riveted to his narrow hips and long, muscular legs.

Then he wrapped the bath towel around his waist. The spell was broken and her cheeks turned as red as American Beauty roses.

"I'm sorry...I didn't...the door wasn't..." she stuttered.

Philippe was amused rather than embarrassed, "You seem so shocked. Is there something about me that's different from other men?"

"No, I..." If he didn't know he was a sublime specimen of manhood, this was certainly no time to tell him! She turned away, mumbling, "I'll let you get dressed." To her consternation, he followed her into her room.

"What did you come to tell me?"

"It can wait," she said with her back to him.

Philippe put his hands on her shoulders and turned her around to face him. "Aren't you making a lot out of nothing? I'm sure you've seen a naked man before."

Not one who made her feel like this, she could have told him. His close proximity and the warmth of his hands on her shoulders were making her legs tremble.

"It's one of those little anecdotes we'll laugh about," he said, coaxing her to share the joke.

She managed a smile. "Maybe *you* will. I'd appreciate it if you didn't remind me."

"Actually, it's a good thing this happened. It adds to our credibility as a married couple. You can work it into the conversation that I have a secret birthmark."

"I didn't see one."

"It's a little crescent-shaped mark here on my groin."

As he reached for the towel, Nicole's hands closed over his. "I'll take your word for it!" she said breathlessly.

"Does that mean you're starting to trust me?" he asked softly.

The situation couldn't have been more provocative. The back of her hand was resting on his warm, smooth skin in an erogenous zone that was dangerously inviting. Nicole knew she should take her hand away, but she seemed unable to.

Philippe drew in his breath as he gazed at her softly curved mouth. "Sweet Nicole," he murmured. "You're so adorable."

He slipped an arm around her waist and drew her slowly toward him. Nicole could have resisted, but she was mesmerized by the light in his gray eyes. She wanted him to hold her close and kiss her without restraint.

For just an instant, Robbie's voice calling from the hallway didn't register. They drew apart as the little boy stuck his head in the door.

"I've been looking in every room for you, Aunt Nicky," he complained.

She gave him a shaky smile. "Well, now you've found me. Did you have fun with Jules?"

"Yes, he's my new best friend. His mother gave us cookies and Jules showed me some neat puppies. Can I have one for my very own, Uncle Philippe?"

"I don't see why not, as long as you take care of it."

"Oh, I will, I promise!" Robbie gave Philippe a

closer look. "You're only wearing a towel. Did Aunt Nicky give you a bath?" The little boy laughed uproariously at his own joke.

"No, but it's something to think about." Philippe slanted an impish glance at Nicole. "I'll see you both later. I'm going to get dressed." He turned at the door. "By the way, Robaire's room is at the end of the hall, next to his playroom."

When they were alone, Robbie chattered on about all the things he'd seen and done with Jules. But for the first time, Nicole didn't give him her full attention.

She was still confused and disturbed by her torrid response to Philippe. It would be different if it was an isolated incident. What woman wouldn't be affected by a real-life Adonis she could reach out and touch?

But she reacted this way under ordinary circumstances. She could feel the excitement when he just entered a room. It was almost as though she was falling in love with him—which would be a disaster! Philippe had only married her to get custody of Robbie. It was a practical decision, nothing more. He would enjoy making love to her, but his emotions wouldn't be involved.

Nicole almost wished she had his lack of scruples. Philippe would be a masterful lover, she thought wistfully. He could rouse her passion in so many ways, with tantalizing caresses, with just the brush of his hard body against hers, with— She was abruptly yanked out of heaven when Robbie tugged on her arm.

"You're not listening to me, Aunt Nicky!"

"Yes, I am, darling." She tried to blot Philippe out

of her mind. "Tell me again about the puppies. How old are they?"

Nicole might have felt better if she'd known that Philippe was facing his own dilemma. He puzzled over it as he pulled on pale-gray slacks and a black turtleneck sweater.

His loins tightened as he recalled how he'd stood before her in full male revelation. A smile tugged at his mouth when he remembered the shock on her face. But there had been something else, too. She'd felt the same desire he had.

Lord, how he'd wanted her! It was a good thing Robaire had interrupted them, because it would have been a colossal mistake for them to make love.

He'd forced Nicole to marry him, and she hadn't stopped resenting him for that. Was she only biding her time, waiting for any excuse to take the boy back to the States? He couldn't afford to become too relaxed with her—which could very well happen if they became lovers.

Sex was out for them, Philippe decided regretfully. He'd like to kiss her everywhere and bury himself in her enticing body, but it would have to remain a forbidden pleasure.

Nicole was self-conscious with Philippe after their traumatic encounter—at least, it had been traumatic for her! But he was so completely natural that she soon got over her embarrassment.

He spent a lot of time showing her around for the first couple of days, starting with the château itself, which was vast. Besides numerous bedrooms and reception rooms, there was a grand ballroom on the third floor. All the rooms were beautifully decorated, with pictures in heavy gilt frames on the walls and exquisite art objects on tables and mantels.

As they walked down a corridor that intersected with another hallway, Nicole remarked, "A person could get lost in this place and never be heard from again."

"Don't worry, we send out search parties on Wednesdays and Fridays," Philippe joked.

He also mentioned a tour of the winery that was close by, but that trip never materialized. After allowing the newlyweds a couple of days to get settled, invitations from Philippe's friends on neighboring estates started pouring in. Everyone wanted to entertain them.

Nicole realized she'd need a complete new wardrobe. Her sewing machine had been sent to the country, but the nearby village didn't have the elegant fabrics she required. Philippe had a ready solution, as he did to most of her problems. He drove her into Paris for the day.

Nicole didn't have to worry about Robbie. He enjoyed playing with Jules. They were always supervised by Maurice or one of the many other château workers, but the boys had a sense of freedom and self-reliance. Nicole had to admit the estate was a wonderful place for a child to grow up.

Philippe drove them into Paris instead of taking the limo and chauffeur. Once they reached the large metropolis, he knew exactly where the shops she wanted were located.

When she commented on his knowledge of the city,

he said, "You'll be equally expert at getting around after you've been here for a while."

How long would that be? she wondered. Philippe sounded as if he expected their arrangement to be permanent. Could they really go on living a lie indefinitely?

The troubling thoughts were pushed to the back of her mind as she looked in the window of a fabric store. The bolts of cloth inspired her as a blank canvas inspires an artist. Nicole couldn't wait to go in and start browsing.

"Why don't you wait for me at one of those chic sidewalk cafés where you can look at all the pretty girls passing by?" she suggested. "You'll be incredibly bored trailing after me in the fabric store."

"I'm never bored when I'm with you." Philippe's eyes lit with laughter. "Aggravated, perhaps, certainly frustrated a lot of the time, but never bored."

"I don't know if you meant it to be, but that's a nice compliment."

"I meant it to be," he answered warmly.

After convincing Philippe to meet her later, Nicole wandered through the shop selecting linen, lace, chiffon and much more. Enough yardage for an entire wardrobe. The time flew by unnoticed. Nicole gasped when she finally looked at her watch. She was terribly late! Philippe would be furious and she couldn't blame him.

She was out of breath when she arrived at the outdoor café where they'd agreed to meet. "I'm terribly sorry!" she apologized. "I completely lost track of time."

"I figured you would," he said with an indulgent smile.

She gazed at him uncertainly. "I thought you'd be angry. I think I would be if someone kept me waiting this long."

"This is your day, *chérie*. I want you to be happy and enjoy it."

"That's awfully nice of you." Even if he was only placating her so she'd be easier to get along with, it was very thoughtful of him.

"The next time you're angry at me, I'll remind you that I do have some good qualities." He looked at her quizzically. "Didn't you buy anything?"

"I got some wonderful fabrics! They were too heavy to carry, so I told the saleswoman we'd pick them up later."

"Then why don't you decide where you'd like to have lunch?"

"Could we stay right here?"

"You just want to ogle all the handsome men passing by," Philippe teased. "I don't know if I like the competition."

Not many men could compete with him, Nicole thought, studying his handsome face as he lifted a hand to summon a waiter. Philippe had everything—looks, charm, grace and great wealth. It was difficult to believe he was her husband—even if it was in name only.

"What would you like to do this afternoon?" he asked while they were finishing lunch.

"Don't you have to get back to work? You've been spending all of your time with me."

"We're on our honeymoon. How would it look if I went right back to work?"

Whenever she started to forget they were just play-acting, Philippe never failed to remind her. "I didn't think of that. You're so good at keeping up appearances," she said mockingly.

He directed a wary glance at her. "I thought we agreed it was necessary for Robaire's sake."

"You're right—as usual."

He took both of her hands in his. "I know this isn't easy for you, Nicole. You miss your friends and your old way of life. That's understandable. If I didn't think this was best for Robaire, I wouldn't ask you to make such a sacrifice."

Nicole realized that very few people would sympathize with her. Here she was in Paris, one of the world's most exciting cities, with Philippe, one of the world's most exciting men. She had a fortune in jewels on her fingers, and she lived in a gorgeous French château, waited on by an army of servants. It was time to stop being difficult.

"You gave up a lot, too," she said. "I guess I can put up with the situation if you can."

"It's a lot easier for me." He raised her hands to his lips. "I get to look at you every day."

An elegantly dressed older couple stopped at their table. They had been sitting nearby and were now leaving. "Excuse us for intruding," the woman said. "We just had to tell you how wonderful it is to see a young married couple so much in love."

"Is it that noticeable?" Philippe asked, smiling.

"You both positively glow when you look at each other," she assured him.

Nicole wondered how the couple knew they were married, then realized they must have spotted her wedding ring.

"I hope you'll be as happy as we've been for the past thirty years," the man said, glancing fondly at his wife.

"You can tell they will be," she said confidently. "They were made for each other. Enjoy your life and have lots of babies," she told them with a twinkle in her eyes. "They'll be absolutely gorgeous!"

When the older couple had moved on, Nicole said, "Imagine being married for thirty years. That's a life sentence!" For once, she was going to make a derisive remark before Philippe did.

His bemused expression hardened. "I guess you can get used to anything." He beckoned the waiter over with the check.

The edgy little exchange between them was baffling. One minute they were getting along, if not like lovers, at least companionably. The next minute they were like racehorses, determined not to let the other get ahead. Why was there always this tension between them? Nicole wondered hopelessly.

It dissipated a short time later in the Louvre. Who could worry about petty problems in the midst of such masterpieces? They wandered through the halls of the stately museum, pausing in front of priceless paintings and epic statuary. Nicole didn't notice when Philippe took her hand; or maybe she took his. It just felt right.

They walked in the Tuileries Gardens afterward and stopped for meltingly delicious pastries and coffee before visiting Notre-Dame Cathedral to look up in awe at the inspiring stained-glass windows.

"You're an awfully good sport," Nicole said on the drive home. "I'll bet you hated doing the whole tourist bit."

"You want me to deny it."

"It would be nice, but I'd know you were only being polite."

"I don't expect you to believe this, but I actually had a very good time today."

"You sound surprised." She laughed.

"Everything about you surprises me. That's what makes you such fun to be with."

Nicole didn't try to analyze the satisfaction his compliments brought. She decided just to enjoy them.

Her pleasure lasted only until they got home. A servant told them Robbie was playing in the garden at the rear of the château, so they went outside, anticipating his excitement at the toys they'd brought back.

An idyllic scene greeted them. Claudine Duval was seated on the grass, holding Robbie on her lap. The sunshine warmed their laughing faces and turned her hair to flaming red, a stunning contrast to the lush green lawn surrounding them.

Robbie called out excitedly when he saw them. "Come on over here! Aunt Claudine is telling me a story."

Nicole felt a pang at how easily the other woman had won his affection. Evidently, no man was immune to her charms, no matter what age he was.

"This is a pleasant surprise," Philippe said. "Why didn't you tell us you were coming?"

Before she could answer, Robbie tugged at her sleeve and said, "You have to finish the story. She was telling me about this French guy that lived a long time ago," he told the other two. "He rode a horse and saved people from the mean guys that wanted to cut off their heads."

Philippe raised an eyebrow at Claudine. "I remember *The Scarlet Pimpernel* as being more adventurous than gory."

"I wanna hear the end," Robbie insisted.

"I'll tell you the second installment next time." When he started to protest, Claudine said, "If I told you the end now, the story would be over. This way, you have something to look forward to."

Claudine was a modern-day Scheherazade. She knew how to keep a male interested. Although in Philippe's case, her methods were undoubtedly more sophisticated, Nicole thought cynically.

Chapter Seven

Nicole just assumed that Claudine would be staying at the château, but fortunately her parents owned a neighboring estate. Claudine was included in all the parties for the newlyweds, of course, so Nicole still saw a lot of her.

One day, Claudine surprised her by dropping over unexpectedly. "I thought we might go out to lunch together, just the two of us," she said. "There's a cute little bistro near here. We can have a leisurely lunch and get to know each other better."

Nicole could think of things she'd rather do—like walking barefoot over broken glass. But she couldn't come up with a graceful way to get out of going. Philippe had gone back to work. Robbie was so busy she scarcely saw him, and Paul's staff took care of the house. All she could do was accept the invitation as graciously as possible.

If Claudine had an ulterior motive in asking her to

lunch, it wasn't immediately apparent. She kept up a running conversation about inconsequential things like clothes and parties on the drive to the restaurant.

Then when they were seated at a table overlooking a charming little pond, they discussed various choices on the menu. Philippe's name didn't come up until after they'd given the waiter their order.

"I suppose everyone has told you how surprised they were that Philippe finally got married," Claudine said.

"Yes, and I imagine you were the most surprised of all," Nicole answered in an equally casual tone.

"I was furious! I couldn't believe he'd do a thing like that just out of the blue. Philippe and I have always told each other everything."

"You must have a very close relationship."

"We do. I hope that won't be a problem between you and me."

"I imagine you and Philippe have discussed that and worked it out," Nicole said with distaste. Did the woman want her to approve of their affair?

"Our friendship is important to both of us. Philippe is very special to me." Claudine paused for an instant. "I don't have to tell you that he was a tremendous catch. Besides being drop-dead gorgeous, Philippe is very wealthy. A lot of the single women in Paris would have liked to be his wife."

"So, why did he marry *me?*" Nicole asked in a brittle voice. "Is that what puzzles you?" If Philippe hadn't told Claudine the truth about their mock marriage, *she* certainly didn't intend to.

"That wasn't what I meant. I can understand why

he'd be attracted to you. What I'm trying to find out is if you love him,'' Claudine said bluntly.

"You think I married Philippe for his money? That's what he and his mother thought when my sister married Raymond.'' Nicole was losing patience. "Is there *any* woman you people think is worthy of a Galantoire?''

"Your sister received really shabby treatment from them. I told Philippe that.''

"A lot of good it did,'' Nicole muttered.

"In his own defense, I have to say that Philippe wasn't necessarily against their marriage. He simply thought they should wait until they knew each other better.''

Nicole made a derogatory sound. "Next you'll tell me his mother is really a kind and gentle soul.''

Claudine laughed. "No, she's not what you'd call warm—or even perceptive. Catherine doesn't realize you have to give love to get it. I feel sorry for her.''

"You're very charitable,'' Nicole said neutrally.

"I can't blame you for feeling the way you do. I've always thought it was a shame that Catherine never got to know your sister. It might have made a difference. Sandra was such a charming girl.''

"You knew my sister?'' Nicole asked in surprise.

"I met her once. Raymond and I were good pals. He brought her over to see me after the big blowup with Philippe and Catherine. I guess he needed somebody sympathetic to talk to. I offered to try to patch things up between Raymond and his family, but he was too angry with them. The whole thing was so sad. Philippe has gone through hell, blaming himself for what happened.''

"He didn't exactly keep an open mind," Nicole said coolly.

"If you feel that way, how could you marry him?" Claudine's eyes narrowed. "For revenge?"

Nicole realized she'd been too candid. She attempted some damage control, choosing her words carefully. "I never expected to fall in love with Philippe. We argued a lot in the beginning. But the chemistry between us was present from the first moment."

"Yes, I know what that's like," Claudine said softly. "The right man can make you forget all the reasons why you shouldn't be together."

Nicole had a feeling of hopelessness as she stared at the beautiful, poised woman across from her. Claudine had everything—charm, assurance, social position. No wonder Philippe was in love with her. The logical question was, what kept them apart?

She asked the other woman directly. "Why didn't you and Philippe ever get married?"

"And ruin our beautiful friendship?" Claudine grinned. Then her lovely face sobered. "Is that why you've been so reserved with me? You thought Philippe and I were lovers?"

"It was a logical assumption. The first question everybody asked him was, does Claudine know you're married? And then when we met, you weren't overly friendly."

"It was nothing personal. I wanted to be sure you married Philippe for the right reasons. I care very much about his happiness."

Nicole was thoroughly confused. Claudine had indicated in so many ways that she was in love with Philippe. Could any woman be selfless enough to give up her lover *and* wish him happiness with somebody else? Or was it possible that she was telling the truth and they were simply close friends, as Philippe had said?

Claudine was looking at her penetratingly. "You never really answered my question. Do you love him?"

"Yes, I do." It was the only acceptable answer.

But after the words were spoken, Nicole had a moment of panic. Was it really true? Philippe could make her nerve ends quiver with just that slow smile of his and the feathery touch of his fingertips on her cheek. It was so easy to pretend to be in love with him in front of his friends. They both gave a great performance. But what if only one of them was acting?

"I didn't really doubt that you loved Philippe. I've seen the way you glow when you're with him," Claudine said. "But I had to be sure. Now that that's out of the way, we can be friends."

Nicole wouldn't have thought it was possible, but she gradually unbent and started to enjoy herself. Before lunch was over, they were laughing and talking together like sorority sisters.

Philippe was already home from his office by the time Claudine dropped Nicole at the château. He came outside to greet the two women, but Claudine merely waved and drove off.

"Paul told me you'd gone out to lunch," Philippe said as he and Nicole went inside. "Did you have a good time?"

"I had a lovely time," she said enthusiastically.

"Claudine took me to L'Auberge de Soleil. The food was wonderful."

"I told you she'd show you around." He opened a paneled door that concealed a well-stocked bar complete with a small refrigerator. "What can I fix you to drink?"

"Perhaps just some sparkling water. I had wine with lunch, and we're going to that big party tonight. I don't want to fall asleep and miss all the fun."

Philippe looked pleased. "I'm glad you're starting to enjoy yourself. Living here isn't so bad, is it?"

"I'm not so sure. If this whole arrangement falls apart, it would be a terrible shock to have to live like a normal person again," she said, only half-joking.

"Why should anything change?" He handed her a tall crystal glass with a slice of lime topping the bubbly water. "Robaire is extremely happy, and you're beginning to feel comfortable here. What could go wrong?"

Just about anything, Nicole thought, considering their precarious relationship. But instead she said, "You might get tired of being married."

"So far I find it very pleasant. It's nice to have somebody to come home to. You're the one who might get tired of the restrictions."

"It's possible." If she really was falling in love with Philippe, their platonic marriage was going to get increasingly difficult. What a disaster it would be if he found out! She forced herself to smile. "Don't worry, though. As I told you, it would be difficult to give up the good life."

"I'll admit I hoped that would influence you," he said slowly. "But I'm not as ruthless as you think. I blackmailed you into marrying me, but I won't pressure you into staying. No matter what you decide, I'll always take care of you.''

In other words, he'd rather she stayed, but he wouldn't be devastated if she left. The frustration that had been building in Nicole suddenly erupted. "That's insulting! I never wanted money from you! I want—'' She stopped, aghast at what she'd almost revealed.

Philippe's long body tensed as he stared at her impassioned face. "Tell me what you want, *chérie*,'' he said softly.

Nicole's long lashes swept her cheeks as she avoided looking at him. "I'm sorry,'' she murmured. "That wasn't very gracious of me, was it? I know you meant well, but I'm quite capable of taking care of myself.''

"I don't doubt that for a moment.'' Philippe's light tone didn't reveal his inner turmoil.

He wanted to take her in his arms and hold her so tightly that their bodies merged into one. She was so enchanting. Lord, how he wanted to make love to her! Philippe was knowledgeable enough about women to know that she'd be receptive. But Nicole wasn't the sort of girl who made love casually. She'd be sorry afterward, and that was unthinkable!

"Well, I guess I'd better start getting ready for the party,'' she murmured.

"You have plenty of time. Tell me what gorgeous creation you've whipped up to wear tonight.''

The charged moment passed thanks to Philippe's ability to smooth over any situation. Nicole relaxed as she described the gown she'd designed.

But when she realized she was going into detail about bias cut and side draping, she said ruefully, "You're an awfully good sport to listen so patiently. I know none of this interests you."

"I'll admit I don't understand all of it, but I like seeing the passion you bring to your work. I do know you're very talented. Claudine loves the gowns you've designed and she knows a lot about fashion."

"She's everything you said she is. I had a great time with her today."

"I knew you would. Everybody loves Claudine." Nicole watched him obliquely. "You two have a lot in common. You come from the same background. You like each other enormously. It seems strange that you never married—each other, I mean."

"Did you mention that to Claudine?"

"Well, yes," she admitted reluctantly.

He looked amused. "I can imagine what she answered." When Philippe saw the doubtful look on Nicole's face, he said, "I don't know how to make you understand the kind of relationship Claudine and I have. She's like a sister to me. There has never been anything romantic between us."

He certainly sounded sincere. Nicole felt a great deal better. "She's such a beautiful woman. I would think she'd have a dozen men buzzing around her, but she came without a date to the last couple of parties."

Philippe shook his head indulgently. "Claudine discards men the way other women change clothes. Her relationship with the latest one is stormy, so I don't know how long he'll last."

Philippe changed the subject after that, but not

abruptly, as though he was afraid of saying too much. They talked about other things until it was time to get dressed for the evening.

Nicole was looking forward to the party that night, especially since she'd found out Philippe and Claudine weren't lovers. It had made her uncomfortable when she thought all of their friends were watching and waiting for her to find out. Everything was working out amazingly well, Nicole thought happily.

The party that evening was a large formal affair, so she'd gone all out, using yards and yards of silver satin brocade. The full skirt swirled below a form-fitting bodice with tiny straps and a deeply scooped neck, front and back. The gown was so cleverly engineered that all she needed to wear under it was a pair of panty hose.

After she'd applied makeup and brushed her hair until it shone, Nicole stepped into her dress. With an approving look at her creation, she reached for the back zipper. It glided up smoothly for several inches, then stopped. She tugged gently, then a little harder, but it wouldn't budge.

Nicole slipped the straps off her shoulders so she could slide the dress around, back to front, to see what the problem was. In her effort to free the zipper, her elbow bumped a vase that was sitting on a slender pedestal. It fell to the floor and shattered with a loud crash.

"Oh, no!" she cried out. It was probably a priceless heirloom! How could she have been so careless?

Philippe came bounding through the connecting

door. He had on trousers, but his dress shirt was unbuttoned. "What happened? Are you all right?"

"No, I feel terrible! I broke your beautiful vase.
Please tell me it isn't irreplaceable."

Nicole was so upset she didn't realize she was nude
from the waist up. The look on Philippe's face alerted
her. His expression had changed in a flash from apprehension to desire. As she fumbled for the top of
her gown, he continued to walk slowly toward her,
devouring her with his avid gaze. She was rooted to
the spot, mesmerized by the white-hot light in his
eyes.

"I knew your body would be this beautiful," he
murmured, sliding his arms around her waist.

She tried to remember all the reasons why this was
unwise, but with his hands caressing her bare back
and his lithe body only inches away, it was difficult.

"Do you have any idea how much I want you?"
His warm mouth slid down her neck. "Seeing you
every day and not being able to touch you like this
has been driving me wild."

She tried desperately to resist him, but her own
desire was racing out of control. "This wasn't supposed to happen," she murmured hopelessly.

"It was meant to be, my darling." He kissed each
corner of her mouth tantalizingly, making her long to
feel his mouth take deep possession of hers.

Nicole's legs felt boneless. She reached out and
gripped Philippe's shoulders for support. The flames
inside her burned hotter when his hands cupped her
breasts and his thumb circled the rosy tips erotically.
With a tiny cry of pleasure, she flung her arms around
his neck and pulled his head down to hers.

"My lovely, passionate beauty," he said huskily. Philippe's gray eyes were incandescent as he surveyed her enraptured face for just an instant before his mouth closed over hers.

Nicole quivered as he parted her lips for a deep kiss that left her clinging to him. While his tongue explored the warm, wet recesses of her mouth, his hands caressed her body sensuously. She shivered but didn't object when he eased her dress over her hips.

Philippe took a step back to look at her, holding her arms out from her sides. She was a provocative sight in only sheer-to-the-waist panty hose, with the gown forming a silvery pool around her ankles.

"You're so exquisite," he said in a ragged voice. "I want to find out what pleases you and bring you more joy than you've ever known." He swung her into his arms and carried her to the bed.

When he joined her there, molding her body to the hard length of his own, Nicole moved against him seductively, letting her breasts trail enticingly across his bare chest.

Philippe caught his breath and drew her hips against his so tightly that she could feel the intensity of his desire. "You do want me, don't you, my angel?"

"Can't you tell?" she whispered.

He buried his face in the scented cloud of her hair and said in a muffled voice, "I've dreamed about this night after night, and now my prayers are about to be answered."

Nicole smiled enchantingly. "We must be in heaven. I can hear bells."

"They're ringing out in celebration." His mouth closed over hers for a drugging kiss.

Gradually, she realized that the telephone was ringing in Philippe's room. When it went on and on, she stirred restlessly. "Someone is trying to get you. Maybe it's important."

"Nothing is more important than you, *chérie.*" He scissored one leg over hers and dipped his head to kiss her breast.

Nicole wasn't inclined to argue with him. She was raking her nails lightly down Philippe's bare back when there was a knock at the door.

"Monsieur Galantoire?" a servant said tentatively.

Philippe raised his head and scowled. "I'm busy at the moment," he called harshly. "Whatever it is will have to wait."

"Yes, sir. I wouldn't have bothered you, but your mother is on the telephone."

"Tell her I'll call her back."

The man hesitated, caught between a rock and a hard place. "I suggested that, sir, but she said she would wait on the line until I found you."

Philippe swore under his breath. "All right, but tell her she will have to wait." He smoothed Nicole's rumpled hair and said tenderly, "I'm sorry, darling. I promise this will never happen again."

"It's all right," she murmured, sitting up and pulling the bedspread over her body.

"You're more forgiving than I am," he commented wryly. "I'll see what she wants and be right back."

"No, don't. Don't come back, I mean." Nicole's

lashes brushed her flushed cheeks as she avoided looking at him. "This wasn't a good idea."

"You don't mean that." He sat on the edge of the bed, facing her. "I don't blame you for being annoyed, but you can't let one little mishap spoil something beautiful between us."

"What just happened was a mistake. I'll admit I was as much to blame as you were, but that doesn't change anything."

"You didn't feel that way a few minutes ago."

How could she deny it? Nicole's cheeks burned at the memory of her unrestrained response to him. "You're very persuasive," she murmured.

"I didn't seduce you, Nicole," Philippe said evenly. "Be honest. You wanted me as much as I wanted you."

"We both realize there is a strong physical attraction between us," she said, choosing her words carefully. "It's a simple matter of chemistry. It can affect people who don't even like each other."

"At least we've established the fact that our— exchange of affection, shall we call it?—was mutual," he said sardonically. "Are you also saying that only sex was involved?"

"What else could it be? The only reason we're married is for Robbie's sake." She glanced at him through her lashes. "It isn't as though either of us wants to make a commitment."

He gazed at her impassively. "You feel we'd be committed if we made love?"

"I'm saying it would change our relationship," she answered hurriedly. "It's never a good idea to let personal issues cloud a business deal."

"Perhaps we should draw up a contract," he drawled. "Just so there won't be any further misunderstandings."

"I think we understand each other," she said steadily.

"Yes, I suppose we do." He stood and looked down at her. "You don't have to worry that I'll test your willpower again. Now that I know how you feel, I'll be sure to knock next time."

Nicole remained motionless, watching as Philippe strode through the connecting door to his room.

She wanted desperately to call him back; her entire body still ached for him. If they hadn't been interrupted, she would be in his arms making love this very minute.

It didn't take much imagination to know what that would be like. She'd already experienced the rush of excitement when their bodies merged and she felt his smooth, warm skin against her bare breasts. Philippe's response had equaled hers. The strength of his desire made her pulse race.

She never would have been able to resist him on her own. Who would ever have thought she'd be grateful to Madame Galantoire for anything? Nicole thought ironically. The woman had done her a favor, though. Yes, Philippe could bring ecstasy, but at what cost?

He didn't pretend to love her. But when he was arousing her to a fever pitch it was easy to forget they had no future together. How humiliating it would be if he discovered she'd fallen in love with him. It was useless to deny it any longer. But she had to be doubly careful from now on and never, ever let herself get into a situation like this again, Nicole told herself.

Chapter Eight

Philippe was in no mood to listen to his mother's recriminations. He told himself not to overreact, but she made it difficult.

"Where on earth have you been, Philippe? I've been sitting here holding this receiver for an unforgivable amount of time!" she complained.

"If you'd let me call you back, you wouldn't have had to wait on the line."

"I'm sorry if it's too much trouble to talk to your mother."

A muscle in his jaw bunched, but he kept his voice level. "What was so urgent that you had to speak to me immediately?"

"Does it have to be a matter of urgency? What were you doing that was so much more important?"

Philippe gave up the struggle with his temper. "I am an adult, a married man. I don't appreciate it when my mother summons me like a little boy, interrupting a conversation I was having with my wife.''

"I might have known you were with that woman! She tried to prevent you from coming to the phone, didn't she?''

"Contrary to what you think, Nicole was happy that you called,'' Philippe answered sardonically.

"Do you expect me to believe that?''

"Frankly, Mother, I simply don't care. Would you like to tell me why you called? Nicole and I are going to a party and I have to get dressed.''

"I knew this would happen! She's turning you against me, just as her sister did with Raymond.''

"Nobody is turning against you,'' Philippe said wearily. "Nicole is a lovely, generous lady. She's made a lot of sacrifices for Robaire. I'm grateful to her, and you should be, too.''

"How is my dear little grandson?''

"He's thriving here in the country. It's a pleasure to watch him grow more self-reliant every day.''

"Then you won't be bringing him back to Paris?'' Catherine asked with a catch in her voice. "When will I get to see him?''

Philippe's irritation lessened. He knew she was feeling lonely and threatened. "We'll be staying at the town house periodically. But you can come here for a visit whenever you like.'' He looked at his watch. "I'm really running late. I'll call you tomorrow, Mother,'' he said before hanging up the receiver.

Nicole would have given anything to be able to skip the party that night, but she knew it wasn't possible. For one thing, it was being given in their honor.

If she didn't show up, Philippe's friends would think they'd had an argument. And if he said she didn't feel well, they'd think she was pregnant—as they already suspected due to the hasty wedding. That was really funny! So why didn't she feel like laughing? Nicole asked herself.

By the time Philippe tapped at her door—the one to the hall, not the connecting door—Nicole had touched up her makeup and brushed her hair. She'd also managed to correct the problem with her zipper so it slid up smoothly.

Philippe looked her over approvingly, without a trace of his recent passion. No one could have guessed what had gone on between them just a short time earlier. Philippe would have enjoyed making love to her, but it obviously wasn't that important to him.

"You look lovely. Are you ready to leave?" he asked. "I'm afraid we're rather late."

Nicole was glad that it was only a short drive to the party. Philippe didn't refer to the earlier incident between them, but she felt more comfortable when there were other people around.

Most of the guests had already arrived, including Claudine, who had come with a date this time. They made a stunning couple. He was as handsome as she was beautiful, a tall blond man with a deep tan and a confident manner.

Claudine brought him over and introduced him as Justin Marchand. "And this is Philippe's charming bride," she said.

"So you're the one who trapped Paris's wiliest bachelor," he said to Nicole with a smile.

"It wasn't an easy job, but somebody had to do it," she answered lightly.

"You've thrown a scare into the entire bachelor population," Justin said. "Philippe was our leader. If he couldn't escape, what chance is there for the rest of us?"

Philippe had joined them in time to hear the other man's lament. He put his arms around Nicole's waist from behind and said, "You have it all wrong. I had to practically blackmail Nicole into marrying me."

She looked up at him over her shoulder. "Not practically. You *did* blackmail me."

"I would have done whatever it took, my love." His arms tightened and he kissed the soft skin behind her ear.

"I never doubted that," she murmured, fighting the treacherous weakness that made her body relax in his embrace in spite of herself.

Nicole glanced away to find Claudine staring at her with an expression very much like envy. Had she lied about her feelings for Philippe? Nicole decided she was imagining things. It had been only a fleeting impression, and it was gone now.

"I guess I'll just have to look on the bright side," Justin was saying. "Now that you're a newlywed you won't have as much time for business. Maybe our wine sales will go up."

"Justin's family winery is a competitor of Philippe's," Claudine explained to Nicole.

"Is your winery near here, too?" Nicole asked him politely.

"It's not far away," he answered. "I'd invite you

to come for a visit, but after you've seen the Galantoire facilities, ours would look primitive."

"Not to me. I've never been to a winery," she said.

"I'll give you a tour of ours tomorrow, if you like," Philippe offered. "I've been wanting to show it to you, but I didn't know if you were really interested."

"It must be nice to be married to a vintner," Claudine commented. "You don't have to send your husband to the store at the last minute if you're having company for dinner. He can just bring a bottle of wine home from the office."

Justin groaned. "Why does everything have to be about marriage?"

"Don't take it personally," Claudine said with an edge to her voice. "It was just an observation. I'm going to get a drink," she announced abruptly before stalking off.

Justin followed her with a weak smile at the other two.

"There's a date that's going to end early," Nicole remarked to Philippe. "When I first saw them together, I thought they made a beautiful couple, but they don't seem to get along very well."

His mouth tightened. "I wish Claudine would stop seeing him."

"Isn't he just a casual date? She's never brought him to any of the other parties we've been to."

"They have an on-again, off-again relationship. Claudine has some wild idea that she'd like to marry Justin."

"She'll have some convincing to do," Nicole said

skeptically. "I could tell from our short conversation that marriage isn't at the top of his wish list."

"She doesn't need to convince anyone to marry her. Claudine is a vibrant, desirable woman."

They were joined by some of the other guests. One of the women looked enviously at Nicole's slender figure. "I love your gown. Don't tell me you made this one, too!"

Philippe drifted off as the women started to talk about clothes.

Nicole smiled and answered their questions mechanically. Her mind was on Philippe. Wasn't his concern over Claudine excessive? Was he jealous of her feeling for Justin? Nicole had a sinking sensation in the pit of her stomach, remembering the expression she'd surprised on Claudine's face. It was difficult to believe they were just friends, but one thing was certain—whatever emotions they felt were mutual.

Philippe returned and took her hand. "If you'll excuse us, I want to show my wife the rose gardens," he told the others.

It was a beautiful night. Moonlight made the white gravel paths sparkle, and the air was scented with the fragrance of roses. As they strolled along a winding path, Philippe said, "You had a beleaguered look on your face. Aren't you enjoying the party?"

"Yes, very much," she answered.

"I was hoping you were starting to enjoy your life here."

"I am—most of the time."

"Then what's wrong? Are you still bothered by what happened earlier?"

"It does make our situation somewhat awkward," she said. Which was quite an understatement!

"I'm not a teenage boy with raging hormones, *chérie*. I can accept no for an answer."

"That's the trouble. I can't pretend that I'm indifferent to you," she said honestly.

"Then I don't see what the problem is. We're married, and the attraction is mutual."

"That's male reasoning for you," she said disgustedly. "I didn't hear the word 'love' mentioned."

His expression was unreadable. "Well, as you Americans say, two out of three isn't bad."

"You might be willing to settle for that. I'm not."

"Then I guess we'll both have to take a lot of cold showers." When she didn't return his smile, Philippe put his hands on her shoulders and turned her to face him. "I want very much to make love to you, but not if you're going to have regrets afterward. I don't want to hurt you, Nicole. You're a lovely, generous lady and I owe you a lot."

Why did he always have to spoil it by reminding her of the reason he married her? Nicole thought hopelessly. That was the insurmountable obstacle between them, not whether he and Claudine were lovers. She could try to win him away from another woman, but she couldn't change sexual attraction to love.

"Well, a party is no place to settle our differences," she sighed. "We'd better go back inside."

Nicole decided to enjoy the party, including Philippe's attention. It gave her an opportunity to demonstrate her own affection—the only prudent way open to her.

He was puzzled, yet pleased when she didn't stiffen

in his arms or turn her head away when he kissed her cheek. Eventually, one of the male guests made a comment.

"You've been married for weeks, Philippe, not days. When is the honeymoon going to be over?"

"Never, if I can help it," Philippe replied, gazing soulfully at Nicole.

Finally, she murmured in his ear, "I think we're overdoing it."

"Actually, I've been practicing restraint." He grinned.

Nicole met Claudine in the powder room a short time later when she went to freshen her makeup. After they'd chatted for a few moments, Claudine said casually, "What do you think of Justin?"

"He's very handsome," Nicole answered without elaborating.

"Yes, but did you like him?"

"He's quite nice as far as I could tell. We only talked for a couple of minutes."

Claudine gazed discontentedly in the mirror. "Philippe doesn't think Justin is right for me."

"It seems to me that's something you should decide for yourself. Does Philippe have to put his stamp of approval on every man you date?"

"No, of course not, but I do respect his opinion."

"Maybe Philippe is lukewarm about Justin because they're business rivals."

"That doesn't have anything to do with it. The Galantoire name is recognized worldwide. Justin's company is more of a boutique winery. They're scarcely competitors. It's a personal thing with Philippe."

"How serious are you about Justin?" Nicole asked in a casual tone.

"I've been thinking about marriage."

Nicole glanced at the other woman out of the corner of her eye. "Did Philippe disapprove of Justin when you two were just dating?"

"No, probably because he didn't think the relationship would last long." Claudine smiled wryly. "I have a short attention span when it comes to men."

Would Philippe approve of her marrying any man? Nicole wondered somberly. She managed to hide her pain at this indication of his unwavering devotion to another woman. "If you're not sure of your feelings for Justin, maybe he *isn't* right for you."

Claudine shrugged. "I have to marry somebody. I'm not getting any younger. I want to have a family before my hair turns gray and people mistake me for my children's grandmother."

"I'm sure you have a few good years left," Nicole joked.

"That's what Philippe says, but he doesn't have to worry. Men get handsomer as they get older."

Nicole thought about Philippe's strong face and virile body. He would look distinguished with silver temples contrasting with his dark hair, and tiny laugh lines at the corners of his gray eyes. They would give his face even more character. Would he still be a part of her life? she wondered wistfully.

The powder room became crowded when two more women came in. Nicole and Claudine went back to the party.

Philippe had been looking for Nicole. "Where have you been all this time?" he asked.

"I met Claudine in the powder room and we got to talking," she said.

"You were together for hours at lunch today. What could you still have to talk about?"

He was smiling, but was that a guarded look in his eyes? Was he afraid Claudine had been indiscreet? "Women never run out of things to say," she answered lightly.

"I'm glad you've found a friend, but I missed you. Are you hungry? There's a buffet in the next room."

"That's why you missed me. You want to get something to eat."

"Now I know we're truly married." Philippe grinned. "You're starting to read my mind."

As they strolled toward the next room, Nicole decided to confront her problem rather than let it make her miserable for the rest of the night. "You certainly have a lot of influence over Claudine," she remarked artlessly. "She's very involved with Justin, but she doesn't want to marry him without your approval."

"If she really knew what she wanted, my opinion wouldn't matter."

"That wasn't the impression she gave me."

"You don't know her very well yet. Claudine always talks things over with me, but ultimately she makes up her own mind—which is as it should be." His attention had shifted to the lavish display of food set out on a gleaming mahogany dining table. "Be sure to try some of the salmon mousse and also the trout in aspic. They're both specialties of the chef."

Philippe didn't seem to have anything on his mind but the buffet supper. If he was worried about losing

Claudine to another man, could he hide his concern this completely?

Nicole didn't know where she stood in the complicated situation, but she decided to put the whole thing out of her mind and just enjoy herself. She certainly couldn't fault Philippe's behavior. Her happiness appeared to be his sole concern.

It was late when they returned home. Nicole went to check on Robbie as she always did, and Philippe went with her.

With his usual thoughtfulness, he'd had the room completely redecorated before they moved to the country. The furniture was child-size, and there were colorful pictures on the walls. Every kind of toy a little boy could want was scattered around the room and spilling out of a toy chest.

Robbie was sleeping like an angel, a stuffed pink elephant in his arms. He stirred and murmured, "I wanna drink of water," when Nicole straightened his covers.

"I'll get it," Philippe offered.

"He isn't awake," Nicole whispered, smiling. "He just says that automatically."

After a few moments, they tiptoed out of the room.

As they walked down the hall, Philippe said, "I never knew little ones could be such a joy."

"I didn't, either," she admitted. "Robbie certainly changed *my* life."

"For the better, I hope," Philippe said softly, taking her hand.

"Oh, definitely," she answered brightly, easing her hand out of his. The subtle mood change between them was unmistakable. "I can't imagine a life without him."

"Even if it means living here with me?"

"How could anyone complain about these living conditions?" she said in a joking tone.

"It's nice to know there is one way I can make you happy—even if it isn't the one I would choose," Philippe added sardonically.

The tension between them was always just under the surface, Nicole thought hopelessly. They were always either on the verge of an argument or of making love.

As they reached her door, she hastily changed the subject. "What time are we leaving for the winery tomorrow?"

"Any time you like. No, wait!" Philippe corrected himself. "I have a meeting tomorrow morning with a man from the county council concerning a zoning change, but I've forgotten when it's scheduled for. Come in my room and I'll check my day planner."

The bedside lamps were on in Philippe's room, casting a soft glow over the turned-down bed. Nicole hurriedly looked away.

For once, Philippe seemed unaware of the provocative atmosphere. He was scanning his schedule. "My appointment is at nine o'clock. It shouldn't take long, so we'll have the rest of the day."

"That's good," she murmured, edging toward the door. "Well, I'll see you in the morning."

"Are you really tired? Stay and have a nightcap with me," he coaxed.

"It's the middle of the night. We should both get to bed."

"That was going to be my next suggestion." He grinned.

"That's what I'm afraid of," she answered lightly.

Philippe stroked her cheek. It was just an affectionate gesture, she told herself, but every inch of her body responded instantly.

"You don't ever have to be afraid of me," he said in a voice like velvet. "I would never hurt you."

Philippe didn't know he already had, Nicole thought somberly. Although it wasn't his fault. You can't make yourself love someone if all you feel is desire.

"Let me bring you the completion we almost shared earlier." He moved closer and cupped his hand around the nape of her neck, under the long spill of shining hair. "Stay with me tonight, *chérie*."

His husky voice made her vibrate like a tuning fork. She could imagine him removing her dress as he had earlier and carrying her to his bed—only this time there would be no interruptions. He would lie beside her, his eyes lighting up the darkness as his fingertips trailed paths of fire the entire length of her nude body.

Philippe urged one strap off her shoulder so he could slide his lips across the swelling curve of her breast. "Let me make love to you, little angel." His mouth dipped lower, tantalizing her with its promise of ecstasy. "I want to possess you completely."

It was a terrible temptation. A wave of yearning swept over her. But Nicole was afraid Philippe would possess more than her body after they'd made love. She couldn't let him own her completely. Not when he didn't love her.

Summoning every ounce of willpower, Nicole stepped back and replaced her shoulder strap with shaking fingers. "It wasn't meant to be earlier, and nothing has changed."

Philippe stared into her eyes for a long moment while she barely allowed herself to breathe. If he kissed her, she'd be lost.

Finally, he said, "All right, no means no, even though I don't agree." He walked her to the connecting door. "But you're just postponing the inevitable. Sooner or later we're going to make love, my beautiful wife," he said softly. "And it will be worth waiting for."

Nicole left him wordlessly and got undressed in a daze. Was Philippe right? Would they make love eventually? And if so, why not now when her entire body ached for him? It was difficult to convince herself that she was doing the right thing.

Sighing deeply, she reached up and turned out the bedside lamp.

Chapter Nine

Nicole's spirits were lighter the next morning. Her relationship with Philippe remained troubling, but there was no point in spoiling the rare day alone with him. Especially since it should be carefree and fun. He could scarcely get romantic at the winery.

Nicole always made it a point to get up and have breakfast with Robbie even if she'd gotten in very late the night before. She felt it was important to start off his morning with a smile and a kiss. He was so involved with various activities that she saw little of him the rest of the day.

Her bright mood dimmed when she and Robbie went downstairs and the butler told them Catherine had come for a visit.

"Madame Galantoire is in the dining room," Paul said. "She is waiting for you and the young master to join her."

"I don't wanna go in there. I wanna eat where we always do," Robbie said.

They had breakfast and sometimes lunch, as well, in a lovely garden room that looked out over manicured lawns and leafy green trees, some of them bright with blossoms or berries.

A child would naturally prefer that to the elegant formal dining room.

"It's good to do something different now and then," Nicole told him. "Remember when you didn't want to have your hair cut in a barber shop? And after the first time, you couldn't wait to go back."

Robbie wasn't convinced that it was the same thing, but he followed her to the dining room without further complaints.

"There he is, my little *bébé!*" Catherine's face lit up when she saw Robbie.

He stuck out his lower lip. "I'm not a baby."

"She didn't mean it that way," Nicole said. "It was a term of endearment—you know, kind of like a compliment. Robbie is getting to be such a big boy, isn't he?" she said to Catherine, hoping to placate both of them.

"I wouldn't know," the older woman answered coolly. "I missed his early years." Her smile returned when she looked at Robbie. "Come give your *grand-mère* a kiss, *chéri.*"

"I don't want to. She smells funny," he said to Nicole in a loud whisper.

Catherine drew in her breath sharply. "That is incredibly rude! Didn't you ever teach the child manners? I'm absolutely appalled!"

"I think he was referring to your perfume," Nicole

said apologetically. "Children are sometimes blunt about what they like and don't like."

"Is that supposed to make it all right?"

"No, of course not." Nicole turned to Robbie. "I want you to apologize to your grandmother for hurting her feelings."

"Why do I have to?" he asked rebelliously. "She said things about *me*."

"That's no excuse. She's your grandmother, and you owe her respect. I don't ever want to hear you speak about her that way again."

"Am I supposed to be impressed?" Catherine asked sarcastically. "I'm not. If you were fit to raise a child, you would have taught him respect for his elders a long time ago."

"See?" Robbie said eagerly. "She isn't nice to you, either. Why do we have to be nice to *her*?"

"I expect you to be polite to everybody," Nicole said firmly.

"Even Sheldon Werby at play school? He put sand in my hair, so I pushed him hard."

Before she could answer, the woman said, "I'm beginning to see why Philippe married you. He didn't trust you to raise Raymond's son the way a Galantoire should be raised."

Nicole was so startled by Catherine's lucky guess that she was speechless for a moment.

"That was your plan all along, wasn't it? To play on Philippe's concern for his nephew. He'd never marry someone like you unless he was forced into it."

"You don't know your son very well." Nicole did

her best to sound unruffled. "Nobody forces Philippe to do anything he doesn't want to do."

"Not under ordinary circumstances, but once a woman lures a man into her bed, he stops thinking rationally."

Nicole was aware of Robbie's anxious expression. "Perhaps it would be better if we postponed this discussion until a more suitable time."

Catherine's face reddened unbecomingly. "You have the *audacity* to tell me what to do?"

"If you're as concerned about your grandson as you profess to be, I shouldn't have to tell you," Nicole said bluntly.

"I see what you're doing. You intend to tell Philippe that I'm a bad influence on the child. You've already turned my grandson against me. Now you're planning to alienate me from my son!"

"I couldn't do that if I wanted to—which I don't." Nicole's anger lessened as she heard the thread of fear underlying the older woman's malice. "Whether you believe it or not, I'm hoping you and I can resolve our differences so we can get along like a nice, normal family. For Robbie's sake, if for no other reason."

"How gullible do you think I am? You've taught the child to ridicule me, and you try to keep Philippe from even talking to me on the telephone. Is that your idea of a family?" Catherine rose and threw her napkin on the table, having worked herself into a rage. "Enjoy your little triumph while you can. You were clever enough to trap my son into marriage, but it won't last. You're not a Galantoire, and you never will be." She swept regally from the room.

Robbie's eyes were enormous. "Why is she so mad at you, Aunt Nicky?"

"She isn't really." Nicole smiled brightly. "Sometimes when adults have a discussion, they just appear to be angry. Your grandmother loves you a lot. It would make her happy if you could be a little nicer to her."

"Do I have to?" he asked plaintively. "I don't like her."

"You can't make up your mind about people until you get to know them better. Now finish your breakfast so you can go out and play." Nicole tried to appear unconcerned in order to minimize the nasty incident.

Throughout the entire argument between the two women, Paul had served breakfast and poured coffee with a complete lack of expression on his face. They could have been speaking a foreign language he didn't understand.

Nicole wondered if Catherine intended to tell Philippe about their disagreement. *She* certainly wasn't going to. It wouldn't be fair to ask him to choose sides between two warring women.

Nicole was alone in the dining room, resting her head on one hand, when Philippe came to look for her.

"Is anything wrong?" he asked.

"No, everything is just dandy." She gave him a bright smile.

"You looked troubled."

"That was a look of concentration. I was dreaming up a new design. Would you like something to eat?"

she asked hurriedly. "I'll have another cup of coffee and keep you company."

"Thanks, but I already had breakfast. Don't you and Robaire usually have yours in the morning room?"

"I like to vary his routine now and then." Nicole paused, reluctant to tell him they had a houseguest. She only hoped that Catherine wouldn't greet Philippe with all of her grievances. It would put him in a bad mood and spoil the nice day they had planned. Well, it couldn't be helped. Suppressing a sigh, Nicole said, "There's something I have to tell you."

"You can tell me in the car," he said. "I want to speak to Paul about something before we leave. I'll meet you out front."

Before she could delay him, he was gone.

Philippe's meeting with the council had gone well. The zoning change meant he could make some long-anticipated improvements to his property, which he wanted to tell Nicole about. They were at least a mile from home before she managed to tell him that his mother was back at the château.

Philippe frowned. "She didn't mention any plans for a visit when I spoke to her on the phone last night. I wonder what prompted this sudden decision."

"Maybe she came to see Robbie."

"That's probably it." Philippe's face cleared. "Then she wouldn't have wanted to come with us today. I'm really looking forward to giving you the grand tour."

The Galantoire winery sat on top of a hill, over-looking the picturesque countryside. A long driveway lined with shade trees wound through vineyards fragrant with grapes.

As they approached the large, graceful building, Nicole remarked, "This isn't at all what I expected a winery to be. It looks more like a country estate."

"Actually, it was a convent many years ago. The tasting room and executive offices are in the front. The real work is done in the back."

The winery itself was dimly lit, cool and quiet. A series of large rooms were filled with huge vats, so tall they had metal ladders fastened to the sides. Philippe pointed out the spigots near the bottom of the casks and told her how the cellar master took samplings at regular intervals. He explained the entire wine-making process, from the crushing of the grapes through the fermentation and distillation.

"You didn't expect such an in-depth lecture, did you?" he finally said with a slight laugh. "You've been such a good audience that I'm afraid I got carried away. Sorry about that."

"Don't be. I found it fascinating," she said. "I'm especially impressed by how knowledgeable you are."

"My father groomed Raymond and me from an early age. We started at the bottom and worked our way up. When Robaire is a little older, he'll follow in the family tradition so he can take over from me someday."

"That isn't a certainty. You might have sons of your own."

"Not unless you're a lot more cooperative." Philippe chuckled.

Nicole didn't allow herself to think of how blissful

it would be to have his child. "Our situation isn't permanent," she said carefully. "I'm sure you want a son. Most men do. You could marry again sometime in the future and have children."

"It's possible, but Robaire will always have an important part in the business."

Nicole felt chilled, and not just from the cool temperature in the fermentation room. Philippe had thought about the future—one that didn't include her. Well, what did she expect? They couldn't go on like this indefinitely.

She was startled when Philippe put his arm around her shoulders. But the gesture wasn't personal.

"Be careful of that puddle on the floor." He led her around a wet spot. "The workers try to keep the floors mopped, but spillage is difficult to see in this dim light. It's easy to slip."

"Yes, it's certainly dark in here."

"I'd explain why we keep it that way, but I think you've had enough technical information for one day."

"I haven't been bored."

"Look me in the eye and say that." He cupped her chin in his palm and raised her face to his.

Nicole melted as she always did at any physical contact with Philippe, no matter how innocent. She stared at his firm mouth, longing to feel it move seductively over hers in a prelude to a passionate kiss that would set her on fire.

Philippe's smile faded as he gazed at her dreamy face. His long fingers stroked her cheek and he murmured, "Sweet little Nicole, you're making it difficult for me to keep my promise. I want to make love to you right here, right now.''

She swayed toward him, unable to hide the fact that she wanted him with the same fervor.

They were both too engrossed to realize they were no longer alone. A worker's footsteps on the concrete floor finally alerted them.

Philippe moved away from her with the poise she always envied. Did he snap back so effortlessly from their romantic encounters because he wasn't affected on the same level that she was? Nicole took a deep breath while he alerted the worker to the spilled wine on the floor by the vat.

As they walked toward the door, Philippe said, ''Now that you know how wine is made, I'll show you the final step before it goes to market.''

Nicole found the assembly line fascinating. The bottles marched down a conveyor belt in single file like little toy soldiers. They stopped briefly to have a cork inserted by a capping machine, then proceeded down the line to the spot where a different kind of machine applied a label.

''It's like a toy factory!'' Nicole exclaimed in delight. ''Robbie would love this. We must bring him here.''

''That's a good idea, but we'll give him an abbreviated tour. He wouldn't be as polite as you've been.''

''I don't know why you say that. You had my full attention.''

''Shall I give you a pop quiz?'' he teased.

''No fair!'' she said, laughing. ''If I'd known you were going to ask questions, I would have taken notes.''

"All right, then, I'll take you to lunch instead. There's a delightful place near here that I think you'll like."

Le Cheval Rouge was a charming little inn with checkered tablecloths and small shaded lamps that cast a soft glow, giving the dining room an intimate atmosphere.

Philippe suggested several dishes that weren't on the menu, specialties of the house that proved to be delicious. He also ordered aperitifs before lunch and wine with their meal.

"I'm not used to drinking this much at lunch," Nicole protested. "I'm afraid I'll fall asleep."

"No problem. They have rooms upstairs. I'll carry you up to bed."

"You don't give up easily, do you?" she asked lightly.

"Do you want me to?" His eyes held hers.

She could say yes, but Philippe knew how he affected her. What he must never know was the extent of her feelings for him. Nicole looked down at the table, concentrating on rolling some bread crumbs into a little ball.

He reached over and covered her hand with his. "I won't try to convince you, *chérie.* I hope someday we'll make love, but only when you're ready—which I hope will be soon," he added with a grin. "Eat your lunch and don't look so serious. I'd hate to have people think we're having a lovers' quarrel when we aren't even lovers."

Philippe dropped the subject after that. Nicole gradually relaxed as he told her amusing stories about growing up in Paris and some of the scrapes he had gotten into. The sexual tension was always present between them; nothing could change that. But they were laughing and joking together like longtime companions. It was an almost perfect relationship. *Almost.* What a difference that one little word made, she thought wistfully.

Robbie was waiting impatiently for them when they returned home, which was a rarity. They usually had to go looking for him, then coax him to come inside. It was a pleasure to see him so involved and happy. That afternoon was an exception.

"Jules had to go someplace with his mother, and I don't have anybody to play with," the little boy complained. "Where did you go?"

Nicole told him about the winery and promised to take him the next time.

"When you get a little older, you can work there like your father and I did," Philippe said.

"What did you do?" Robbie asked.

"We started out sorting the grapes before they went down the conveyor belt to the crushing machine. Raymond and I ate so many that we almost lost our jobs." Philippe chuckled.

"I could do that," Robbie said eagerly. "I'm four already. That's pretty old."

"You're right," Philippe agreed solemnly. "Well, we'll see when crushing season comes around." He paused as the butler entered the den.

"Madame Galantoire said to tell you when you returned that she wishes a word with you."

"I suppose I should tell her we're home," Philippe

said with some reluctance after Paul had left. "Robaire, why don't you run upstairs and ask your grandmother to join us in the den?"

The little boy looked at Nicole. "Do I have to?"

Philippe frowned. "I wish you would be a little friendlier toward your grandmother. She came all the way from Paris just to be with you."

"I don't care. I don't like her. She talked mean to Aunt Nicky."

Philippe's gaze sharpened as he looked at Nicole. "You never mentioned it. Why didn't you tell me?"

"It was nothing," she said dismissively. "Robbie just misunderstood."

"No, I didn't," he insisted. "She got all red in the face, then she said Uncle Philippe doesn't trust you. And then she said you lured a man in your bed. I don't know what that means, but she looked like it was something bad."

Nicole was appalled at how much of the nasty argument the child had understood. Maybe not completely, but too close for comfort.

Philippe's square jaw set rigidly. "You should have told me about this," he said to Nicole. "My mother has stepped way over the line this time! I can only apologize and assure you it will never happen again."

"See?" Robbie said triumphantly. "Uncle Philippe says I'm right!"

"He didn't say that," Nicole corrected him hurriedly. "You gave him the wrong impression. I told you we were only having a discussion." Before the little boy could argue the point, she said, "Go upstairs and get ready for your bath. I'll be up in a minute to wash your ears.''

They both waited until he had left the room. Then Philippe said, "How could you keep something like this from me? You knew I wouldn't put up with it.''

Nicole shrugged. "What good would it do to start a big family row? It would only make your mother dislike me more—if that's possible,'' she added wryly.

"She can damn well be civil to you!''

"She's only here for a visit, so why start World War 3? Maybe she'll go back to Paris soon.''

"It wouldn't surprise me, not after the talk I intend to have with her,'' he said grimly.

Nicole rose. "Robbie's waiting for me, so I'd better go. At least promise you won't lose your temper.''

"I'll try not to.'' That was as far as he would budge.

Nicole felt flattered at Philippe's outrage on her behalf, but his mother would make things unpleasant for all of them if he was too blunt with her. She sighed and went into Robbie's room.

Nicole usually hung up his clothes and put away his toys while he bathed, talking to him from the bedroom and looking in on him occasionally. But that day, she pulled up a stool and encouraged him to talk about Jules and the puppies, anything to erase Catherine's accusations from his mind.

She needn't have worried. A four-year-old's memory is fleeting at best. Robbie was more interested in telling her about a birthday party he was invited to and showing her how his rubber duck popped up when he submerged it under water.

By the time his bath was over, Nicole was glad she'd made a quick change into jeans and a T-shirt. She was soaked to the skin. While Robbie was playing in his room, she went into her own room to put on dry clothes.

Nicole was just about to strip off her wet T-shirt when there was a knock at the door. "Who is it?" she asked warily, not wanting to go another round with Catherine.

"It's Philippe. May I come in?"

She hesitated. "Can you come back in about five minutes?"

"This won't take long. I just want to verify something before I speak to Mother."

Nicole stopped worrying about her disheveled appearance and went to the door. This was more important than how she looked. Was Philippe going to disregard her advice?

He didn't seem to notice at first that she'd changed clothes. Striding restlessly around the room, he said, "I was thinking about what Robbie said. Did Mother actually tell you that I don't trust you?"

"Not exactly. She said you didn't trust me to raise Robbie like a Galantoire should be raised." Nicole smiled ironically. "You can't be angry at her for that. You said the same thing when we first met."

"And I was just as mistaken." Philippe came over and put his hands on her arms. "That was before I knew what a kind, caring person you are."

"I kept telling you, but you wouldn't believe me," she joked.

"I had to find out for myself." His fond expression changed to something more intense as he gazed at her.

Nicole suddenly realized that her wet T-shirt was plastered to her breasts, leaving nothing to his imagination. The pink tips were almost as clearly visible as if she were nude.

Trust Philippe to show up whenever she looked unintentionally sexy. This was the way he'd seen her the first time they met—and it was still just as embarrassing!

When she started to cross her arms over her breasts, Philippe's hands tightened, preventing her from concealing herself. "Let me look at you, darling. Your body is so beautiful."

"I have to change clothes and take Robbie downstairs for his dinner," she murmured, trying to sound convincing.

"It's still early." His hands slipped under the hem of her shirt and caressed her waist before moving up with tantalizing deliberation.

Nicole made a tiny sound of delight when his fingertips stroked her breasts sensuously and circled her taut nipples.

"I can't stay away from you," he groaned. "I know I'm only torturing both of us, but when I see you like this, I can't help myself."

"I can't, either," she whispered. Every erotic encounter was fueling her need for this man, chipping away at her resolve.

"I shouldn't be doing this to you." But instead of moving away, Philippe drew her close and buried his face in her hair.

The heat he was generating burned away her inhibitions. She dug her fingers into his rigid buttocks and pulled his hips even closer to hers. He uttered a hoarse cry and arched his back, making her even more aware of his raging desire.

While his mouth hungrily possessed hers, he slid both hands inside her waistband and cupped her bottom, lifting her into the juncture of his hardened loins.

"We can't stop now," Philippe said in a ragged voice.

"I know," she whispered, pulling his shirt out of his slacks.

"Darling girl, this is like a dream come true," he murmured as he unzipped her jeans.

They were so engrossed in each other that at first they didn't hear the sounds coming from Philippe's room. The peremptory knocking became insistent and Catherine's voice could be heard, muffled but unmistakable.

"Philippe? I know you're in there. Open this door!"

"I don't believe it!" Philippe exclaimed, raising his head and staring at Nicole. "This is the second time she's done this to us."

Her body protested against the intrusion as strongly as his. Every instinct told her to ignore it. Then sanity returned, and she took a deep breath.

"These interruptions aren't accidental." She fastened her jeans with shaking fingers. "Your mother is trying to keep us from making love." Nicole laughed bitterly. "That's kind of funny when you think about it."

"It's also unrealistic. She can't check on us all night."

"Maybe the servants told her we don't sleep together—in the same bedroom, I mean. She might think our marriage is in trouble and she's trying to make sure we don't repair it.''

"I know she hasn't become reconciled yet to the fact that we're married," Philippe said slowly. "But I don't think she'd try to break us up."

"I'm sure she thinks it's in your best interests, but it's time you made your mother face some hard facts." The frustration that filled Nicole made her more caustic than she would normally have been. "If our marriage falls apart, Robbie's custody is once more up for grabs. I realize you have unlimited wealth to fight for him, but don't think it will be a slam dunk. I'll play the sympathy card and every other trick I can think of.''

Philippe's expression changed. "He's really the only one you care about, isn't he?"

"Robbie's welfare is the reason we got married," she answered indirectly. "I agreed to your terms because I didn't have any choice."

"But you had no intention of getting further involved." He smiled mockingly as he headed for the door. "I almost slipped under your guard a couple of times, including tonight. Too bad you recovered in time. It would have given me a great advantage.''

Nicole felt as though he'd slapped her. She'd managed to keep her true feelings hidden, but he was being honest. Philippe wouldn't have passed up a chance to make love to her, but not because of any deep longing. His secret agenda was to make her emotionally dependent on him.

How could she continue the mockery of their marriage? But what else could she do?

Chapter Ten

Nicole forced herself to go down to dinner that night although she dreaded having to face Philippe and his mother. For once, luck was on her side. Paul informed her that Philippe had gone out and—equally good news—Catherine had returned to Paris.

He must have had a frank discussion with his mother and told her to lighten up or else. It didn't give Nicole any satisfaction. Philippe hadn't done it for her sake.

The next few days were easier than she expected because Philippe left for Paris, ostensibly on business. That meant they didn't have to attend the endless round of social events. Nicole was urged to come without him, but she made up various excuses.

Surprisingly, Robbie missed his uncle. He'd grown accustomed to Philippe by now, but Nicole hadn't realized how much a part of the little boy's life Philippe had become.

"When is he coming home?" Robbie asked. "He was gonna take me and Jules fishing."

"Maybe Jules's father can take you," she suggested.

"No, he has to work. Besides, I want Uncle Philippe. He tells me all kinds of neat stories about stuff he did when he was a little boy."

"I'll tell you stories."

"I already heard all your stories."

Nicole had the bleak feeling that she was being edged out of Robbie's life. Philippe could provide everything the child needed. Once he realized he'd gained Robbie's affection, her usefulness would be over.

Nicole told herself she was indulging in self-pity. Robbie depended on her for a lot of things. A child needed both a mother and a father figure in his life.

All the same, it was time she got on with her own life. She should have been working harder on her designs. What with one thing and another, she'd completed very few sketches since they moved to the country. If her marriage unraveled—as all the signs indicated—she needed a career to fall back on.

Philippe returned in time for the weekend, which delighted Robbie, at least. He and Nicole were sitting on the terrace playing Go Fish when Philippe arrived. The adults greeted each other politely, in contrast to the little boy, who raced over to hug his uncle's legs enthusiastically.

"Did you bring me something?" he asked eagerly. "Mommy and Daddy always brought me a present when they came home from a trip."

"Paul took my luggage inside. Ask him to give you

the shopping bag I brought.'' Philippe ruffled the child's hair fondly.

''Oh, boy!'' Robbie tore into the house.

Nicole rose and prepared to follow him, not wanting to be alone with Philippe.

''Don't go,'' he said. ''I have a present for you, too.''

''That wasn't necessary.''

''I couldn't let our one-month anniversary go by without some recognition.''

''Has it only been a month?'' she exclaimed.

''I know it seems much longer,'' he said mockingly.

It did seem longer, but not the way he meant. The past seemed very distant since Philippe came into her life and gave it color and excitement.

''Consider this a consolation prize,'' he drawled, taking a blue velvet box out of his breast pocket and handing it to her.

Inside was a diamond-and-sapphire pin in the shape of a bird. Its eyes were cabochon sapphires, and the wings were a combination of the two kinds of jewels, only these were faceted, so they sparkled brilliantly in the sunlight.

''It's gorgeous!'' she gasped. ''But you really shouldn't have. I mean, under the circumstances...'' Her voice trailed off.

''Because of our difference of opinion the other night? You simply reminded me of the reason you married me. The chemistry is so strong between us that I tend to forget that on certain occasions. Even you, the steel butterfly, were guilty of a lapse of memory.'' His mouth curved derisively.

"Please, Philippe," Nicole murmured. She couldn't bear to be reminded of the paradise that kept eluding her.

"I could tell our desire was mutual," he continued in spite of her protest. "So I couldn't understand your reluctance. I'm glad you were finally honest with me."

"You act as if I was guilty of some kind of deception. You married me for the same reason I married you."

"That's true. You're a lot more pragmatic than I am. It's a mistake in any business relationship to get emotionally involved."

"I agree," she said stiffly.

"Now that we've cleared the air, you don't have to worry about any future incidents. Unfortunately, we still have to act like a loving couple in public, but that shouldn't be difficult since we both know it's just a necessary evil."

Nicole didn't think she'd ever been more miserable. They weren't even friends anymore. Philippe considered her a business partner—one he'd get rid of in a heartbeat when the time was right.

Fighting for composure, she held out the velvet box. "I can't accept this."

"You deserve it after all you've had to put up with."

"I never expected this job to be easy," she answered coolly.

"Then consider it a prop in our little playlet. You can wear it to the brunch on Sunday."

Nicole was momentarily distracted. "What brunch?"

"Surely you haven't forgotten," he said sardonically. "The Clermonts are giving a champagne
brunch in honor of our one-month anniversary. We
have to go. We're the guests of honor."

"Will your friends ever stop celebrating our marriage?" Nicole asked hopelessly.

"Not until somebody else gets married or makes
the news another way. They need some reason for
their endless round of parties. I thought you were enjoying them."

She was, until things went so wrong with Philippe.
In the beginning, it had been merely an annoyance
when he teased her by hugging and kissing her in
public, knowing she couldn't object. Now it would be
torture.

Robbie returned carrying a gift box filled with
brightly colored, but unidentifiable, pieces of a toy.
"I tried to put this together, but the pieces don't fit.
I didn't break it," the little boy said anxiously as he
handed the box to his uncle.

"Let's see what we can do about it." Philippe sat
cross-legged on the flagstone and took the pieces out
of the box.

"What is it supposed to be?" Nicole asked.

"I hope it will be a fire truck." He was reading
the instructions. "How do they expect kids to assem-
ble these things? You need an engineering degree."

"You can do it, though, can't you, Uncle Philippe?"

"*Certainement.*" Philippe grinned at the little boy.
"In English that means you can count on it."

Robbie's worried expression eased as he brought
the box over to show Nicole the picture. "Uncle Phil-

ippe is really neat! He can do anything," he said confidently.

Philippe raised his head and gazed at Nicole for a moment. "Well, almost anything."

After the toy truck was assembled, he showed Robbie how to activate the siren and make the ladders go up and down.

Robbie was ecstatic. "I wanna show Jules. Will you come with me? I mean, right now!"

Nicole had a lump in her throat as she watched the tall man and the little boy walk away hand in hand. This made it worth all the pain. Her sister's son was the important one after all.

Nicole wore narrow white silk pants to the brunch, topped by a powder-blue cashmere sweater to match the diamond-and-sapphire pin Philippe had given her. She'd pinned it to the sweater. It was easier than arguing about it. What difference did it make anyway? It wasn't as though the pin had any sentiment attached.

Philippe noticed it instantly, but he didn't comment. All the women at the party did, however.

"I adore your brooch," Monique, their hostess, exclaimed. "It's absolutely gorgeous!"

"Thank you." Nicole managed a smile. "Philippe gave it to me for our one-month anniversary."

"That's so romantic! I hope you know how lucky you are to have a husband like Philippe."

"Nicole expressed her feelings, I can assure you." His eyes sparkled with hidden amusement as he urged her rigid body close to his side.

"A diamond pin would bring that reaction from any woman," one of the men observed cynically.

"Not Nicole," Philippe said. "Her reactions are always unexpected."

"That's supposed to be the key to a happy marriage," François, the host, commented. "Always keep your mate guessing."

"Philippe knows exactly how I feel about him," Nicole drawled, turning her face up to his. Two could play at that game!

He retaliated by holding her closer and kissing the corner of her mouth. "Very few marriages are like ours."

Claudine arrived, creating a merciful diversion. As always, she looked stunning in a designer outfit that showcased her excellent figure.

Philippe left their group immediately and went over to say hello. So much for his idyllic marriage, Nicole thought sardonically. He and Claudine had a short private conversation before a couple of the other guests joined them.

Some time later, Nicole met up with Claudine in a summerhouse on the grounds. The brunch was being held outside on the vast manicured lawns of the Clermont estate.

"You look terrific," Claudine told her.

"You do, too. Is that an Escada you're wearing?" Nicole asked.

"You really know your designers."

"That was the business I was in. I recognize their work even if I can't afford their prices," Nicole joked.

Claudine looked surprised. "You can now."

"Well, uh, yes, that's true. But I guess I pinched pennies for so long it got to be a habit. Is Justin here with you today?'' she asked quickly to change the subject. ''I haven't seen him.''

"No, and you won't. Justin is history.''

"That's too bad. He was very good-looking.''

"It isn't enough,'' Claudine said dismissively. ''Justin has too many hang-ups for me. I guess Philippe spoiled me for other men.''

Nicole was speechless. For the first time, Claudine was admitting that she and Philippe had been more than friends.

"You don't know how fortunate you are,'' she continued.

"That's what everybody keeps telling me.'' Nicole tried for an amused tone but didn't quite succeed.

Philippe approached without either of them noticing. He came up in back of Nicole, put his arms around her waist and kissed the soft skin in back of her ear.

"What are the two most beautiful women at the party talking about?'' he asked.

"You should have been here,'' Claudine told him. ''I was telling Nicole that I'm looking for a man exactly like you.''

"Did she offer to hand me over?'' Philippe asked lightly.

"That would be too much to hope for,'' Claudine answered in the same jesting tone.

François approached, holding up a jeroboam of champagne. He was followed by a servant carrying a tray of glasses.

"Everybody gather around,'' François called. ''We

have to toast the happy couple before brunch is served.''

People drifted over to form a circle around Philippe and Nicole and their hosts. After all the glasses were filled, François made the first toast, a nice tribute to love and marriage. Then the guests joined in. Some of the toasts were sentimental, some slightly ribald.

Finally, François said, ''Now it's time to give the guests of honor a chance. Philippe?''

Philippe looked deeply into Nicole's eyes and said, ''I want to thank my lovely bride for making me realize what I've been missing all these years. I will always owe her a debt of gratitude for enriching my life.''

Someone took the glass out of his hand as he folded Nicole in his arms. She responded instantly and without conscious thought. When his mouth closed over hers, everyone else ceased to exist. She was in a magical world where Philippe loved her, only her, and they would live happily ever after.

Her compliance brought a low sound of pleasure deep in his throat. Philippe was as oblivious to the others as she was. Sliding his mouth across her cheek, he murmured in her ear, ''You're so sweet and natural. You make me ashamed of myself.''

There was applause after Philippe's toast, then some joking comments when they showed no signs of drawing apart. Finally, Philippe, at least, became aware of their audience. He released her reluctantly.

While he fended off the good-natured teasing, his murmured words finally registered with Nicole.

Why was Philippe ashamed? For trying so relentlessly to seduce her? Or because he'd never broken off his affair with Claudine? Was Philippe taking advantage of both of them?

When she looked up at him doubtfully, he smiled and kissed the tip of her nose. "My bride is too polite to say so, François, but I think she's getting hungry."

"Thank heavens!" Monique exclaimed. "I didn't like to interrupt the toasts, but the chef is having a nervous breakdown in the kitchen. His soufflés are almost ready to come out of the oven."

They all drifted over to the round tables that had been set up on the lawn. Each table was covered with an embroidered yellow organdy cloth, centered by a bowl of fragrant tea roses. The crystal compotes at each place setting, filled with strawberries, black raspberries and mango slices, made the tables even more colorful.

It wasn't your average brunch, Nicole reflected— but nothing about her life was average since she'd married Philippe. Waiters continued to pour champagne, while more waiters served individual cheese soufflés, plus a number of other delicacies.

Everyone was in a jovial mood. In the general hilarity, nobody except Philippe noticed that Nicole was unusually quiet.

"I'm sorry this is such an ordeal for you," he said in a low voice. "We'll leave as soon as brunch is over."

"It isn't an ordeal," she said quickly.

"You don't have to pretend with me. I know you too well by now."

"I wonder if a man and a woman ever really know each other?" She sighed unconsciously, thinking of their lack of trust in each other. His suspicion was unwarranted. Was hers?

"People have a better chance of knowing each other if they talk things out instead of losing their tempers," Philippe said. "I'm referring to myself."

She couldn't help smiling. "My temper is rather volatile, too."

"You see? We have a lot in common." His laughter died as he said, "I did a lot of thinking about us while I was alone in Paris. We both—" He paused as Claudine gestured from across the table to get their attention.

"We'll finish our discussion later," Philippe murmured to Nicole.

After brunch, the guests wandered around the beautiful grounds while the tables were being cleared. Philippe's plan to leave early was foiled by their hostess.

"The entertainment will start shortly," she announced. "You're all going to love this magician I found."

"At least two of us aren't going to stick around to find out," Philippe muttered.

"Be polite," Nicole scolded. "Monique went to a lot of trouble for us. We can't possibly leave now."

"I suppose you're right." He took her hand and led her away from the others, into a patch of woods that bordered the lawn. "I'd like to clear things up between us as soon as possible, though. As I started to say at the table earlier, I'm sorry about our quarrel the other night. I said a lot of things I didn't mean."

"People often tell the truth when they're angry," she said quietly.

"The only truth is, it came as a shock to find out

you still regard me as the enemy. That's why I over-reacted. You should know I'd never try to cut you off from Robaire, no matter how our personal relationship turns out." He stroked her hair gently. "Even if we're not lovers, we can still be friends."

Nicole fought against the spell Philippe could weave so easily. "Friends don't use sex to gain an advantage," she said harshly. "You said yourself it would have given you leverage."

"That's just one of the many stupid things I've said to you." He framed her face in his palms and gazed deeply into her eyes. "You have to know how much I want to make love to you, *chérie*. When I kiss you and touch your exquisite body, do you honestly believe I'm thinking of anything except how blissful it would be to bury myself inside you?"

Nicole's heart thundered in her breast as she remembered his seductive hands caressing her sensuously while his mouth drove her wild with desire.

"We've had a lot of misunderstandings, but they aren't insurmountable. I'm willing to do whatever it takes to mend our relationship. I want you to be as happy as I've been since you came into my life," he said in a husky voice.

She looked at him uncertainly, wanting to believe, yet afraid of being hurt again. "Whenever we're getting along, something always happens to spoil it."

"Most marriages are rocky in the beginning, darling. It's only natural when two formerly independent people live together. But we have a special incentive to make our marriage work. We're raising a child together, a little boy we both love."

Nicole could no longer doubt his sincerity. Budding happiness started to unfold inside her like a beautiful flower. "I'm willing to give it another try if you are," she said with a bubbly little laugh.

"My darling wife!" Philippe folded her in his arms, but with tenderness rather than passion.

As Nicole relaxed against him and inhaled the clean male scent of his skin, Monique called from the distance, "The show will start in about ten minutes."

Nicole and Philippe drew apart reluctantly. When they started back, she noticed Claudine standing at the edge of the lawn, staring at them intently. Something about her fixed gaze made Nicole uncomfortable. She might have mentioned it to Philippe, but they were stopped by one of the male guests who wanted a word with him.

While they were standing on the lawn, a light breeze sprang up, ruffling Nicole's hair. She discovered one of her earrings was gone when she brushed a strand of hair off her cheek. The earring probably fell off when Philippe was cradling her face in his hands, she thought, smiling in remembrance. With a murmured excuse, she left the men and went back into the woods.

The piece wasn't valuable, but the earrings had been a gift from a dear friend. Nicole was determined not to lose it. After searching the path without success, she went into the denser underbrush. She was crouched down, examining the leaf-strewn ground when she heard Claudine's voice, followed by Philippe's.

Nicole didn't intend to eavesdrop—at least, it wasn't a conscious decision. But their first words left her stunned.

"Couldn't this have waited?" Philippe asked with a trace of impatience.

"How can you be so insensitive?" Claudine exclaimed. "Haven't you noticed how miserable I've been all day?"

"I'm sorry, *chérie*," he said in a softened voice. "I know what you're going through, but everything will work out."

"You keep saying that, but nothing happens! When I saw the way you looked at Nicole just now, I wanted to cry."

"Your time will come," he said soothingly.

"When? I don't want to spend the rest of my life alone."

"You won't ever be alone, my dear. I'll always be here for you."

Nicole was in shock. Philippe had staged the whole reconciliation scene with her just a few minutes ago—right down to the same husky voice and soulful glances.

And she'd fallen for it! She'd believed him when he said he'd do anything to make her happy. Of course he would, Nicole thought bitterly. If he kept her happy, she'd be content to stay married to him and wouldn't make trouble over Robbie.

And all this time, the one he really cared about was Claudine. His only problem was convincing the other woman that patience was a virtue. But that was only a minor problem for a man like Philippe. He had awesome ways of convincing a woman.

But not this woman, not anymore! Philippe had deceived her for the last time. Nicole's eyes were bleak as she faced a future without him. Then she squared her shoulders and lifted her chin. She would survive.

Chapter Eleven

After a sleepless night, Nicole made a wrenching decision. She had to go back to San Francisco and try to pick up the pieces of her life. It broke her heart to leave Robbie, but he would be better off in France. Philippe might not love any woman, but he loved his nephew. And the child had grown to love him. Philippe could charm the devil himself, Nicole thought hopelessly.

She would phone and write to Robbie regularly. And maybe when the bitterness faded, Philippe would let him come visit her. She could never come back here.

But she had the present to deal with right now. Her face was pale, yet composed when she went downstairs to talk to Philippe. It wasn't going to be easy.

He'd known something had gone wrong at the brunch yesterday. Nicole had pleaded a sudden headache, which didn't satisfy him. She did look drawn, though, so he didn't pester her with questions. She braced herself now for the coming battle.

Philippe reacted with shock to the news that she was leaving. When she told him why, he was incredulous.

"You can't still be jealous of Claudine! What does it take to convince you that there is nothing romantic between us? I thought you finally believed me."

"Like I believed everything else you told me?" she asked bitterly.

"What has happened to upset you, *chérie?* Tell me and I'll make it better," he said in a honeyed voice, moving toward her.

"Don't touch me!" Nicole's body was rigid. As disillusioned as she was with him, Philippe had a way of melting the ice around her heart.

"At least tell me what's wrong," he pleaded.

"I heard your private conversation with Claudine at the party yesterday. I was in the bushes, looking for the earring you knocked off during that touching scene where you told me how much our marriage meant to you. You were so convincing that I didn't realize I'd lost it."

"Not *that* convincing, evidently. You must have had some lingering doubts about my sincerity or you wouldn't have been listening in the bushes."

"Don't try to make *me* the guilty party! You're the one who's been playing games from the moment you found out about Robbie. I might be able to condone that, but trying to make love to me so I wouldn't ask awkward questions about your private life was despicable!"

Philippe looked at her impassively. "You've decided that was my motivation?"

"Don't try to tell me it wasn't. I heard you tell Claudine that everything would work out and she wouldn't be alone."

"Is that what this is all about?" he exclaimed. "You misunderstood completely! I was only—"

"You needn't bother to think up a creative explanation," Nicole interrupted. "I wouldn't believe you even if you told the truth—which would be a novelty."

His jaw set. "I can tell that nothing I say will change your mind. What excuse do you intend to give Robaire?"

"I'll think of something." She steeled herself not to let her misery show.

"You can really just walk away without a backward glance?" he asked slowly.

Why would he mind? The answer was simple—because he wanted a stable home for Robbie and no problems over his custody. "I have to pack," she said. "Will you have someone drive me to the Paris airport?"

He gave her a startled look. "You're leaving today? You don't even know if you can get a seat on such short notice."

"If I can't get a direct flight to San Francisco, I'll go through New York. There are always a lot of planes leaving for there." Nicole was anxious to end the conversation. She didn't know how long her composure would last.

But Philippe delayed her maddeningly. "What

about your career as a dress designer? My offer of help still stands.''

Her few sketches weren't nearly polished enough to take to a couturier. She could tell herself that she'd been too busy with Robbie, but the truth was that her life with Philippe had been so full there was no room for anything else.

As she hesitated, looking for an answer that wouldn't reveal too much, the doorbell rang. A moment later, Paul ushered Madame Galantoire into the den.

"Don't worry, I'm not staying," she told Philippe sarcastically. "I just stopped by to pick up my jewelry case. I was so upset by your boorish behavior that I left without it."

"I'm sure you had more jewelry at home," he drawled. "You didn't need to make a special trip."

"You don't have to make it so insultingly clear that I'm not welcome in this house," she said angrily.

"That wasn't my intention. I merely meant you could have saved yourself the long drive."

"I had to be in the neighborhood anyway. I'm meeting a group of friends for a tour of the winery and luncheon afterward. I'm leaving as soon as I get my case."

"You might want to spare a moment to say goodbye to Nicole before you go. She's returning to San Francisco."

Nicole had hoped he wouldn't tell his mother until after she'd left. But Philippe was determined to exact revenge.

The delight Catherine didn't bother to hide was

tempered almost immediately by concern. "You're not going to let her take Robaire?"

"Couldn't you be gracious just for once? Nicole has generously offered to give up custody of the boy. She and her sister have shown a lot more understanding toward the Galantoires than they've ever received from us."

"I don't like your tone, Philippe! None of this is *my* fault."

"No, I have to share the guilt," he sighed.

"It's pointless to assign blame or indulge in recriminations," Nicole said impatiently. "At least we all want what's best for Robbie. That's why I'm leaving him with you. Just don't let him forget me." Nicole turned away abruptly as tears clogged her throat. "I have to pack."

The other two were silent for a moment after she left. Then Catherine began hesitantly, "Perhaps I could have been more—"

Philippe cut her off. "It's too late, Mother." His eyes were bleak.

Nicole had put off telling Robbie she was leaving, knowing it would be traumatic for both of them. But after her suitcases were packed and she'd checked all the dresser drawers twice to be sure she hadn't forgotten anything, the ordeal couldn't be postponed any longer.

Philippe was still in the den where she'd left him. He was simply standing at the window, staring out at the grounds. Nicole gazed at his taut body, cherishing this last glimpse of him. In spite of everything, she couldn't stop loving him.

When Philippe turned and saw her, she looked away hurriedly. "I'll be ready to leave after I say goodbye to Robbie. Will someone be available to drive me?"

"I'll take you," he said.

"No!" How could she bear to be cooped up in a car with him, close enough to touch, yet forever beyond her reach? "I mean, you must have things to do. If you can't spare anyone, I'll get there somehow."

"Do you hate me that much, Nicole?" he asked quietly.

"I didn't say that! It's a long ride and you probably have appointments scheduled," she said carefully, not wanting their final parting to be contentious. "Don't feel you have to see me off."

"Why not be honest? You can't even stand to look at me."

It was true in a way. How could she look at his handsome face and know she'd never feel his seductive mouth on hers again? Nicole could feel her resolve weakening. Wouldn't it be easier to pretend to believe his lies so she could share at least a part of his life?

She drew a deep breath, resisting the self-destructive temptation. "I don't want to argue with you, Philippe. I'd like to leave on a civilized note."

Before he could answer, the front doorbell rang in a series of urgent peals. Philippe frowned and strode into the hall to answer it before Paul could get there.

A workman in coveralls stood on the doorstep. "There has been an accident, Monsieur Galantoire.

You must come immediately. Your mother has been injured.''

"How? What happened?" Philippe exclaimed.

"The cellar master was giving Madame and her friends a tour of the winery. She slipped on a patch of wet floor and gashed her neck badly. A metal bolt was protruding from one of the wine vats. There was much blood.''

"Where is she now?" Philippe asked tautly.

"An ambulance was called. It took her to the hospital. You should go there quickly, monsieur. Madame is very frightened.''

"I'll go with you, Philippe." Nicole had followed him into the hall.

He paused for an instant. "You don't have to feel obligated. I know you're in a hurry to leave.''

"What kind of person do you think I am?" she asked indignantly. "I wouldn't leave you at a time like this.''

Emotion choked his voice as he said, "I continue to underestimate you.''

They spoke very little on the short ride to the hospital. Philippe was tense, and Nicole couldn't reassure him that everything would be all right. Catherine's injury sounded grave. The best she could do was put her hand on his sleeve sympathetically. He squeezed her hand hard and gave her a grateful look. It wasn't the emotion she wanted, but at least they were friends again, briefly.

Catherine was in the emergency room when they reached the hospital. The doctors and nurses surrounding her looked grave. The doctor in charge came over to them and explained the older woman's condition. She'd sustained various minor bruises, but the gash to an artery was the one they were concerned about.

"But she'll recover, won't she?" Philippe was very pale.

"The problem is that she's lost a lot of blood," the doctor answered indirectly. "Your mother needs an immediate blood transfusion. Unfortunately, her blood type, AB negative, is very rare. Only one percent of the population has that blood type."

"Are you telling me there is none available?" Philippe demanded.

"Not here. We can get some from Paris, but it will take time. I'm not happy about the delay."

Nicole had hesitated to interrupt but now she said, "I'm type AB negative. I'll gladly donate blood."

"That's splendid!" the doctor exclaimed. "Nurse! We've found our donor. Take care of this young woman."

While everyone was bustling around getting the equipment ready, Philippe clasped Nicole's shoulders. "You would do this for a woman who has caused you nothing but misery?"

"I would do it for any human being in need," she answered simply. "When it's a case of life or death, you don't dwell on your grievances."

"Oh, darling!" Philippe folded her in his arms. "It's no wonder I love you so much."

Could she really have heard correctly? Nicole wondered. He was too distracted to be playing games here in the hospital—which had to mean he was telling the truth!

Nicole was in a kind of daze as she followed a nurse into another room.

After she'd given blood, the woman brought her a glass of orange juice and advised her not to get up immediately as she might feel a trifle unsteady.

Nicole felt more than a little disoriented, but it wasn't from giving blood. She had to talk to Philippe and find out if he meant what he said. A sudden thought chilled her. Maybe it had been just an extravagant expression of gratitude.

Philippe wasn't alone in the waiting room when Nicole ignored the nurse's order and went to join him. Claudine was there with Justin, which was odd since she'd said she wasn't interested in him any longer.

"You're a heroine!" Claudine exclaimed when she saw her. "Philippe told me how you saved the day."

"You look pale, darling." He gazed at Nicole with concern. "Are you all right?"

"I'm fine," she said, hiding her despair. What more proof did she need that Claudine was the most important woman in Philippe's life? They had an idyllic relationship. All he had to do was tell her he needed her, and she came instantly. "You must have been shocked when Philippe called you about the accident," she said numbly to the other woman.

"Philippe didn't call me. One of Catherine's friends did. She wanted me to phone and tell her if Catherine was going to be all right. The hospital wouldn't give them any information. I rushed right over, naturally."

"It was nice of you to come with her," Philippe said to Justin.

"He's been hiding a lot of good qualities. This

might not be the ideal time, but I have to tell you both the big news. Justin and I are getting married!''

"It's about time you made up your mind." A smile relieved Philippe's stress as he shook the other man's hand. "Claudine was ready to give up on you."

"That's what did it," Justin said. "When I thought about a life without her, I knew it wouldn't hold any joy."

Nicole felt slightly light-headed as he and Claudine talked excitedly about their plans. Had Philippe been telling the truth all along? But what about the things she'd seen and heard with her own eyes and ears?

Finally, he noticed how quiet she was. "Nicole shouldn't be standing here like this. She needs to lie down."

"Of course," Claudine said with compunction. "I just wanted to check on Catherine and see that you were holding up okay. Take care of Nicole. You're a lucky man!" She hugged her warmly.

After the other couple had left, Philippe inspected Nicole's pale face closely. "Perhaps I'd better call the nurse."

"No, I just have to sit down for a minute." She stared at him uncertainly as he led her to a couch and sat beside her. "Are you really happy about Claudine and Justin? I thought you didn't like him."

"I was annoyed with him because he was making Claudine—and himself—miserable out of sheer pig-headedness. They're mad about each other, but Justin refused to marry her because she's so much wealthier than he."

"They didn't really act as if they were in love," Nicole said doubtfully. "Claudine seems a lot fonder of you than Justin. She even came right out and told me you'd spoiled her for other men.''

"People have a smoother relationship when they aren't in love." Philippe smiled.

Nicole wanted to believe him and let it go at that, but she couldn't. "There have been so many indications that you two are a great deal more than friends," she said slowly. "I overlooked them, but the final proof was yesterday when Claudine cried in your arms and said she didn't want to spend her life alone.''

"Is that why you decided to leave?" Philippe exclaimed incredulously.

"You don't have to explain," Nicole said quietly. "We didn't have a real marriage. I couldn't expect you to be faithful to me.''

"Whether you believe it or not, I have never been unfaithful to you, not with Claudine or any other woman." He gazed into her eyes steadily. "I hoped we could make our marriage work even though you kept reminding me that you only married me because of Robaire.''

"You married me for the same reason. I was always afraid you'd try to get sole custody of him.''

"Do you honestly think I would do anything that cruel?" he asked reproachfully. "You must really hate me.''

Nicole's long lashes fluttered down. "You know I don't," she murmured.

"I know I can arouse you, but you never really wanted to make love," he said sadly.

If he only knew how wrong he was! "A lot of things that happened between us were...misunderstandings," she began haltingly. "I guess I misjudged you part of the time, but it's still difficult to believe your relationship with Claudine is strictly platonic. I *heard* you tell her she wouldn't be alone, that you'd always be there for her."

"I did say that, but it didn't mean what you think. What advice did I give her?" he prompted.

"I don't know. You both walked away and I couldn't hear any more. I didn't really want to," Nicole said somberly.

"That's too bad. You would have heard me tell Claudine that Justin would come around if she stopped trying to convince him to marry her and simply gave him an ultimatum. I figured that would shock him into proposing."

"*You* gave her the idea?"

He shrugged. "She'd tried everything else. If he was stupid enough to let her go, then it was time for her to get on with her life. You simply heard me reminding her that she wouldn't be alone, no matter what Justin decided. True friends are always there for each other."

Nicole felt as though a huge weight had been lifted from her heart. Days and nights of misery could have been avoided if she'd just trusted Philippe!

"You look tired, *chérie.*" He squeezed her hand gently. "I'll take you home."

"Not yet. Let's wait until we're sure your mother will be all right. Neither of us would feel comfortable leaving before then."

Philippe agreed, but he made Nicole lie on the couch in the waiting room even though she assured him that she was fine. He brought her the orange juice she was supposed to drink and was so solicitous that her heart brimmed with joy.

The doctor finally came out to tell them Catherine's vital signs were good and he expected her to make a full recovery. She'd been given a sedative, so he suggested they leave now and phone later to check on her condition. The inference was clear: the doctor didn't want Catherine to have visitors for a while.

As Philippe and Nicole walked to his car he said, "I know this has been an ordeal for you. I want to get you home and into bed as soon as possible."

"You've been trying to do that since I got here."

"I only meant..." Philippe paused as she grinned mischievously. He chose his next words with care, afraid of saying the wrong thing. "I never made any secret of my feelings, but it didn't do me much good."

Nicole smiled enchantingly. "I didn't think you'd give up so easily."

"You'll never know how hard it was! But I thought that's what you wanted."

"Just tell me one thing. Did you mean it when you said you love me?"

"More than I ever thought it was possible to love anyone!" He took her in his arms and held her so tightly that he was almost a part of her. "Don't leave me, my dearest one. I'll do anything to make you happy. You don't have to love me, just let me love *you*. How can I live without you?"

"I'm not going to let you find out." She gazed up at him with shining eyes. "Darling Philippe, don't you know you're the love of my life?"

Incredulous joy replaced the strain on his face. His

mouth closed over hers for a kiss that held equal parts of yearning, passion and tenderness.

When he finally released her, she sighed happily. "It's hard to believe that two people who love each other could have so many misunderstandings. We need to have a long talk."

"We'll get around to that, too." His sultry gaze made her heart soar. "Let's go home, *chérie*."

Nicole and Philippe walked up the stairs of the château hand in hand. It was like being in a dreamworld. But when they reached her room and he took her in his arms, Philippe's hard body proved unmistakably that he was very real.

"I've waited so long for this," he groaned, tangling his fingers in her silken hair and tilting her head back so he could string a line of burning kisses down her neck. "I thought it would never happen."

"I felt the same way," she said faintly. It was difficult to talk with Philippe's plundering mouth trailing a fiery path to the valley between her breasts.

He had unbuttoned her blouse and was nuzzling the curves that swelled about her lace bra. Nicole's anticipation mounted as his fingers slipped inside the wispy garment to stroke her breasts erotically.

When she closed her eyes and moved sensuously against him, Philippe said huskily, "You're finally going to be my wife in every way."

He removed her clothes in a matter of seconds, then gazed avidly at her nude body. The naked desire on his face made her legs tremble.

"Don't be shy with me, darling," he said as her long lashes brushed her flushed cheeks. "I want to know every exquisite inch of you and I want you to know me the same way.''

He removed his own clothing with a complete lack of embarrassment. He had nothing to be self-conscious about, Nicole reflected. Philippe had the lean torso and long, muscular legs of a champion athlete.

She moved closer and ran her palms over his broad chest, then continued down to his flat stomach. His warm skin felt wonderful under her hands, inviting further exploration. But when she reached his loins and stroked his bursting manhood, Philippe uttered a hoarse cry and pulled her hips tightly against his.

''I want this to be good for you, but you're testing my staying power,'' he said, breathing rapidly.

''We've both waited entirely too long already.'' She smiled dreamily, swaying her hips suggestively.

''I couldn't agree more.''

While his tongue parted her lips for a deep, drugging kiss, Philippe swung her into his arms and carried her to the bed. Without letting her out of his arms, he covered her body with his and wound his legs around both of hers.

Their bodies were almost welded together by the heat they were generating. Nicole's excitement mounted almost unbearably as Philippe's tongue flicked in and out of her mouth while he caressed her intimately.

''I need you so,'' she gasped, parting her legs.

''That's what I wanted to hear!'' He entered her, burying himself inside her.

His deep penetration brought such joy that she cried out his name. Philippe held her close as their bodies pulsated with pleasure. They moved against each other, faster and faster in a dance of delight that spiraled to unbelievable heights.

When they reached the summit, a cresting wave of sensation rocketed through their taut bodies, relieving the tension. The gentle downward spiral left them feeling drained, yet completely fulfilled, content just to lie in each other's arms.

Finally, Nicole stirred and gazed at him. "I've always dreamed about what my wedding night would be like, but I couldn't have imagined anything this wonderful," she said softly. "I love you, Philippe."

His arms tightened convulsively around her. "I'll never get tired of hearing you say it. I thought I'd lost you forever when even Robaire couldn't keep you here."

"He was the excuse I gave myself for staying— even after he adjusted so nicely. But when things went so wrong between us, I had to admit he would be happy with you even if I wasn't here."

"We would both have been inconsolable." Philippe stroked her cheek tenderly. "He needs both of us, so why don't we adopt him legally? Are you ready to consider it now?"

"I think it's a great idea!" Nicole smiled bewitchingly. "I know that's something I'm good at. I have more experience as a mother than I do as a wife."

"I look forward to remedying that." He trailed sensuous patterns over her bare bottom. "We might even think about giving Robaire a little brother or sister."

Philippe's child! The thought of it was dazzling. "I'd like at least one of each," she said breathlessly.

"Then we shouldn't waste any time." His hand
slid up the inside of her thigh.

She drew away with great reluctance. "We have to
call the hospital, Philippe."

His face sobered and he glanced at the clock on
the nightstand. "You're right. Mother might be awake
by now."

Philippe picked up the phone and was soon con-
nected to Catherine's room.

After asking how his mother was feeling and hearing the doctor's report, Philippe was surprised when
she asked to speak to Nicole.

"I want to thank you." Catherine's voice sounded
hesitant, not at all the imperious tone she usually used
toward Nicole. "The doctor told me what you did for
me."

"It was nothing," Nicole said dismissively. "I just
happened to have the right blood type."

"No, we both know it was an uncommon act of
generosity. I don't expect you to forgive me for the
inexcusable way I've treated you, but I want to apologize anyway. I just wish I could offer the same apology to your sister."

"You've been through a bad experience," Nicole
said slowly. "We can talk when you're feeling better."

"You think the sedatives have left me confused,
but you're wrong. This accident has made me realize
how selfish and narrow-minded I've been. You made
my son happy. That's what any normal mother hopes
for. I can't ask you to overlook my behavior, but I
want you to know I'm sorry—for everything."

Nicole had a lump in her throat. "Every family has

misunderstandings, but they get over them. We have more important things to think about—like Robbie. Philippe and I are going to adopt him. I'll let Philippe tell you about it.'' She handed over the phone.

After Catherine and her son had concluded their conversation, he said to Nicole, ''She was thrilled by the news.''

Nicole gave him a rather stunned look. ''I can't believe she's the same woman.''

Philippe grinned. ''An epiphany will do that to you sometimes. At least something good came out of her accident. The doctor says she'll recover nicely, so let's get back to the subject we were discussing.'' He molded her nude body to his and twined their legs together.

''I have a feeling it won't be a long conversation.'' She laughed.

''There are times when words aren't necessary.'' Philippe's smile faded as he looked deeply into her eyes. ''You must know by now how much I love you.''

Nicole didn't get a chance to voice her own love, but she didn't need to. The kiss they exchanged was a promise neither would ever break.

* * * * *

Look Who's Celebrating Our 20ᵗʰ Anniversary:

Celebrate
20
YEARS

"Happy 20ᵗʰ birthday, Silhouette. You made the writing dream of hundreds of women a reality. You enabled us to give [women] the stories [they] wanted to read and helped us teach [them] about the power of love."

—*New York Times* bestselling author
Debbie Macomber

"I wish you continued success, Silhouette Books.... Thank you for giving me a chance to do what I love best in all the world."

—International bestselling author
Diana Palmer

"A visit to Silhouette is a guaranteed happy ending, a chance to touch magic for a little while.... It refreshes and revitalizes and makes us feel better.... I hope Silhouette goes on forever."

—Award-winning bestselling author
Marie Ferrarella

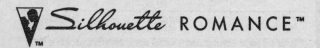

Silhouette ROMANCE™

Visit us at www.romance.net

PS20SRAQ1

SILHOUETTE'S 20ᵀᴴ ANNIVERSARY CONTEST
OFFICIAL RULES
NO PURCHASE NECESSARY TO ENTER

1. To enter, follow directions published in the offer to which you are responding. Contest begins 1/1/00 and ends on 8/24/00 (the "Promotion Period"). Method of entry may vary. Mailed entries must be postmarked by 8/24/00, and received by 8/31/00.

2. During the Promotion Period, the Contest may be presented via the Internet. Entry via the Internet may be restricted to residents of certain geographic areas that are disclosed on the Web site. To enter via the Internet, if you are a resident of a geographic area in which Internet entry is permissible, follow the directions displayed on-line, including typing your essay of 100 words or fewer telling us "Where In The World Your Love Will Come Alive." On-line entries must be received by 11:59 p.m. Eastern Standard time on 8/24/00. Limit one e-mail entry per person, household and e-mail address per day, per presentation. If you are a resident of a geographic area in which entry via the Internet is permissible, you may, in lieu of submitting an entry on-line, enter by mail, by hand-printing your name, address, telephone number and contest number/name on an 8"x 11" plain piece of paper and telling us in 100 words or fewer "Where In The World Your Love Will Come Alive," and mailing via first-class mail to: Silhouette 20ᵗʰ Anniversary Contest, (in the U.S.) P.O. Box 9069, Buffalo, NY 14269-9069; (In Canada) P.O. Box 637, Fort Erie, Ontario, Canada L2A 5X3. Limit one 8"x 11" mailed entry per person, household and e-mail address per day. On-line and/or 8"x 11" mailed entries received from persons residing in geographic areas in which Internet entry is not permissible will be disqualified. No liability is assumed for lost, late, incomplete, inaccurate, nondelivered or misdirected mail, or misdirected e-mail, for technical, hardware or software failures of any kind, lost or unavailable network connection, or failed, incomplete, garbled or delayed computer transmission or any human error which may occur in the receipt or processing of the entries in the contest.

3. Essays will be judged by a panel of members of the Silhouette editorial and marketing staff based on the following criteria:

   Sincerity (believability, credibility)—50%

   Originality (freshness, creativity)—30%

   Aptness (appropriateness to contest ideas)—20%

   Purchase or acceptance of a product offer does not improve your chances of winning. In the event of a tie, duplicate prizes will be awarded.

4. All entries become the property of Harlequin Enterprises Ltd., and will not be returned. Winner will be determined no later than 10/31/00 and will be notified by mail. Grand Prize winner will be required to sign and return Affidavit of Eligibility within 15 days of receipt of notification. Noncompliance within the time period may result in disqualification and an alternative winner may be selected. All municipal, provincial, federal, state and local laws and regulations apply. Contest open only to residents of the U.S. and Canada who are 18 years of age or older, and is void wherever prohibited by law. Internet entry is restricted solely to residents of those geographical areas in which Internet entry is permissible. Employees of Torstar Corp., their affiliates, agents and members of their immediate families are not eligible. Taxes on the prizes are the sole responsibility of winners. Entry and acceptance of any prize offered constitutes permission to use winner's name, photograph or other likeness for the purposes of advertising, trade and promotion on behalf of Torstar Corp. without further compensation to the winner, unless prohibited by law. Torstar Corp and D.L. Blair, Inc., their parents, affiliates and subsidiaries, are not responsible for errors in printing or electronic presentation of contest or entries. In the event of printing or other errors which may result in unintended prize values or duplication of prizes, all affected contest materials or entries shall be null and void. If for any reason the Internet portion of the contest is not capable of running as planned, including infection by computer virus, bugs, tampering, unauthorized intervention, fraud, technical failures, or any other causes beyond the control of Torstar Corp. which corrupt or affect the administration, secrecy, fairness, integrity or proper conduct of the contest, Torstar Corp. reserves the right, at its sole discretion, to disqualify any individual who tampers with the entry process and to cancel, terminate, modify or suspend the contest or the Internet portion thereof. In the event of a dispute regarding an on-line entry, the entry will be deemed submitted by the authorized holder of the e-mail account submitted at the time of entry. Authorized account holder is defined as the natural person who is assigned to an e-mail address by an Internet access provider, on-line service provider or other organization that is responsible for arranging e-mail address for the domain associated with the submitted e-mail address.

5. Prizes: Grand Prize—a $10,000 vacation to anywhere in the world. Travelers (at least one must be 18 years of age or older) or parent or guardian if one traveler is a minor, must sign and return a Release of Liability prior to departure. Travel must be completed by December 31, 2001, and is subject to space and accommodations availability. Two hundred (200) Second Prizes—a two-book limited edition autographed collector set from one of the Silhouette Anniversary authors: Nora Roberts, Diana Palmer, Linda Howard or Annette Broadrick (value $10.00 each set). All prizes are valued in U.S. dollars.

6. For a list of winners (available after 10/31/00), send a self-addressed, stamped envelope to: Harlequin Silhouette 20ᵗʰ Anniversary Winners, P.O. Box 4200, Blair, NE 68009-4200.

Contest sponsored by Torstar Corp., P.O. Box 9042, Buffalo, NY 14269-9042.

ENTER FOR A CHANCE TO WIN*

Silhouette's 20th Anniversary Contest

Tell Us Where in the World You Would Like *Your* Love To Come Alive... And We'll Send the Lucky Winner There!

Silhouette wants to take you wherever your happy ending can come true.

Here's how to enter: Tell us, in 100 words or less, where you want to go to make your love come alive!

In addition to the grand prize, there will be 200 runner-up prizes, collector's-edition book sets autographed by one of the Silhouette anniversary authors: **Nora Roberts, Diana Palmer, Linda Howard** or **Annette Broadrick**.

DON'T MISS YOUR CHANCE TO WIN! ENTER NOW! No Purchase Necessary

Silhouette®
Where love comes alive™

Visit Silhouette at www.eHarlequin.com to enter, starting this summer.

Name:

Address:

City: State/Province:

Zip/Postal Code:

Mail to Harlequin Books: **In the U.S.:** P.O. Box 9069, Buffalo, NY 14269-9069; **In Canada:** P.O. Box 637, Fort Erie, Ontario, L4A 5X3